# Books by Emma Rose Lee

## The Tales of the Nez Percé

**Mustang Eyes**

**Black Wolf**

*Bear Claw coming soon*

## The Elwood Legacy series

The Slaves of Zachavi

The Girl of Glander *coming soon*

Ten years down the road and now it is finally published, thanks to two lovely people.

Sarah Vogel

Mel Mather

I couldn't have done it without them.

"….For *The Lord does* not *see* as man sees; for man looks at the outward appearance, but the Lord looks at the heart."

- I Samuel 16:7 NKJV

# The Slaves

# Of

# Zachavi

*Emma Rose Lee*

# The Legacy of Elwood

# Part 1

The Legacy of Elwood

# Chapter 1

A girl in a deep scarlet cloak ran swiftly through the castle gates, through the pouring rain, toward the royal stables—someplace where she could get some quiet time and not be so overwhelmed with royal business.

The girl was plain, but pretty, with her forest-green eyes and gleaming red-brown hair. Her only turn-off was her skin, which was an unusually dark shade of beige; she was one to be out in the sun a lot.

Her name was Ranaya Yarkish, the princess of Lakishea.

She'd had more than enough of obtuse conversations about this and that, about politics, wars, marriages, and countless other topics with her parents and others of high class. Why couldn't she be normal like other girls her age? The peasant girls never had to endure all the things she did. They didn't have to wear awful corsets that cinched their middles and stole away their breath; they could wear perfectly comfortable clothes and not have to be concerned about appearances. Peasant girls could go out in the sun and not have to worry about getting too much of it; it didn't matter to them. Instead of endless talks of politics, their sole concern was household duties.

The stable was the only place where the princess could escape the tide of regal duties, where she could get at least a moment's peace and be able to think clearly.

She was good friends with all the stable hands and sometimes helped them with their chores even though they insisted this was unfit work for a princess; she would only laugh and roll her eyes at them. When she wasn't in the castle, she was very unladylike; sometimes she would go so far as to dress in men's clothes. She was a fan of riding astride a horse, with a leg on each side; it was so much more comfortable and convenient than riding sidesaddle.

When she reached the stable, there was no one in sight. How strange, she thought to herself as she settled onto a fresh hay bale, prepared to stay awhile.

Unfortunately, only a few minutes later the butler came to fetch her. "Your father wants to see you in the throne room," was all he told her, and then waited for her to follow him.

Oh, she could never escape!

Grudgingly, Ranaya got to her feet, walking back into the castle with an unladylike scowl. That scowl only deepened when she entered the throne room where her father stood with another man, also apparently of high class.

"Ranaya, this is King Karik of Zachavi," her father, King Darius, said with a bow.

*Zachavi!* Ranaya almost staggered at the name.

Zachavians were known to be a highly racially prejudiced folk. They tried to eliminate all the elves in the area, and in the surrounding areas beyond. So far as Ranaya was concerned, Zachavians were no more than filthy murderers.

Ranaya could never understand their mad hatred for elves. After all, elves weren't much different from anyone else. Granted, there were their prominently pointed ears, and they were considerably more attractive as well, and their culture differed slightly. But the Zachavians believed the elves used their good looks to lure their victims into deadly traps in the forest. The Lakisheans, thankfully, were much wiser than that and didn't believe in a particle of that nonsense.

The truth was, the mysterious disappearances in the Tarachi Forest had nothing to do with the elves. The Tarachi Forest was a dangerous place, where anyone could get lost easily— and if there were any traps, surely they were meant purely for catching animals rather than humans.

"Greetings, Your Majesty," Ranaya said to King Karik with a stiff curtsy, wondering as she did what this man was doing there and what his purpose was.

He wasn't half-bad-looking. He had sleek black hair, which was pulled back stylishly, and piercing brown eyes. He was quite young, somewhere between his late twenties and early thirties. Yet despite his attractiveness, there was a sinister air about him. He didn't look like the sort of man you would want to make angry.

Karik bowed to her in return, just low enough to be polite. "I am here for important business with your father," he said.

His tone was civil enough, yet there was a cool edge to it that sent a slight shiver down Ranaya's spine.

"What sort of business?" Ranaya quirked an eyebrow.

Why was she here if this business didn't involve her?

Clearing his throat, Darius spoke up. "Well, daughter, it will certainly involve you later on. I just thought you would like to meet Karik, since he will be staying with us a while."

Ranaya sighed, knowing what her father must be thinking. She was eighteen now and therefore at an suitable age to marry. Her father was most likely trying to engage her to this king. Well, if that was the case, he needn't bother, because she wasn't going to marry anyone, least of all the king of the Zachavians. Doubtless he was the source of the raging fire of prejudice that engulfed the realm.

"I see." Ranaya shot Karik a brief yet intense glare that let him know what she really thought of him, then she quickly left the room, returning to the stables once more.

If Darius thought he could just marry his daughter off to this so-called king, he had another thing coming. "Of all the nerve!" Ranaya shouted irately, kicking a hay bale across the stable hall.

"Your Highness!" a scolding voice sounded right then. She gave a start, then realized it was just Harry, the stable manager, whose pointed nose gave him the resemblance of a hawk, but who wasn't that bad-looking otherwise. "That is no way a lady of your class should act," Harry said reproachfully, picking up the bale Ranaya had just kicked and setting it back to its former position, which Ranaya thought was utterly ridiculous since they were in a place where hay was scattered everywhere.

"Harry, do you realize what my father is doing right now?" She frowned, then dropped her gaze to the dirt floor and sighed. She didn't like being called "Your Highness" in the stables, but no matter how many times she told Harry and the others, they still referred to her by that title, so it did no good.

"No, Your Highness. What has happened?" Harry asked, genuine concern now showing in his face and tone. His lady's sudden change of mood wasn't like her at all.

"My father—or should I say, Darius Yarkish—is handing me over to some king of Zachavi. For all I know, this sort of thing has been predetermined since the day I was born. My life isn't really my own!" Agitatedly, Ranaya began to pace the floor. "A Zachavian, of all people! The filthy racists that they all are!" She felt her face flush. Even if that last statement wasn't entirely true, she knew it couldn't be far from the truth. She blinked rapidly, fighting to keep back the tears gathering in her eyes.

Harry didn't know how to respond. With his lady being so upset, he didn't want to say the wrong thing. Then remembered the new stable hand he'd hired just that day. Perhaps he could cheer her up and change the subject at the same time.

"May I have the liberty of introducing you to my newest stable hand? A handsome lad he is, and not much older than yourself." Harry winked at Ranaya, who wiped at her face, feeling mortified.

Ranaya sighed. *Too bad I can't marry a stable hand,* she thought miserably. *It would be so much better than a racist king!*

Footsteps sounded behind them. Ranaya turned to see a young man only a few years older than her approach. He was strikingly handsome, with blonde hair that fell casually to his shoulders, covering his ears. He had intelligent eyes as blue as the sky, and he was tall and lean, yet sturdy. Ranaya blinked, then turned to look back at Harry.

"Your Highness," he said grandly, "meet Lando."

He had said the lad was handsome, but "handsome" was a major understatement. This 'lad' was not ordinary.

"Nice to meet you, Lando." Ranaya curtsied awkwardly, in a rather un-princess-like way.

"The pleasure is all mine, Your Highness." Lando smiled and bowed politely in exchange. Compared to Ranaya, his grace was astonishing.

Ranaya had to fight the temptation to roll her eyes. "Please, call me Ranaya," she told him, trying to not sound bossy.

"Yes, Your—Ranaya." Lando caught himself in time.

He never called a royal by their Christian name. It wasn't proper, but if she insisted… well, he had better obey.

"So Lando, where are you from?" Ranaya loved learning things about the stable hands.

Lando cleared his throat. "If you please, I prefer to not speak of my past." His cheery tone and countenance became troubled. He looked down at his boots.

Ranaya decided it might be best to not ask any more questions, for the time being. She understood and respected other people's privacy as much as her own.

"Well, Lando, I think it's time to start your training," Harry cut in. He tilted his head ever so slightly toward the supply room.

"Yes, sir," said Lando courteously.

"And you, missie, need to go back to your own world and tend to your own business," said Harry to Ranaya, shooing her away playfully.

She sighed, but chose not to argue.

This granted her a perfect opportunity to have a little talk with her father. She needed to speak to Darius about the whole ordeal with Karik and try to find some way out of it— if it was possible.

Ranaya knew, even before she had reached the throne room, that her father and Karik were discussing her. *Just what I expected,* she thought when she heard their voices and could distinguish their words. *Well, I'm going to tell them something they would never expect!*

She put on a smug, simpering look as she pushed through the heavy oaken doors and went in. Darius and Karik looked up at the same time, both looking surprised to see her.

"Back so soon?" Darius inquired as Ranaya sauntered over to them.

Ranaya just shrugged as she glanced briefly at Karik. Just the sight of him alone was enough to turn her stomach.

"Father, I must speak to you," she said, focusing her gaze on him. "At once."

"If you must, by all means, go ahead," Darius said, rather snidely.

"Alone," said Ranaya, dropping her voice to a whisper. "Not in front of *him.*"

Karik grinned, and Ranaya resisted the urge to slap it right off his face.

Darius cleared his throat. "Excuse me," he said crisply to Karik as he took his daughter by the arm and they went out into the hall. As soon as they were alone, he demanded impatiently, "Now, what is it you wanted to speak of, daughter?"

"I am *not* marrying that sorry excuse for a king!" It was all Ranaya could do to keep her temper, to avoid ending the sentence with a stamp of her foot like a spoiled child. She would rather die than be wed to someone who was so prejudiced, who tortured and murdered for the pure fun of it.

"You are, and you will," said Darius firmly, crossing his arms. Darius was a very stern and stubborn father; he always did what he thought was best for his child, what he considered to be good and fair.

It was never good and fair for Ranaya.

"No, I am not! Why don't I ever get a say in the matter? I don't want to be the wife of the man whom I despise above all others!" Ranaya was always known for having a very short temper, and could easily explode like a lit firework.

"I am only doing what is best for you, what is best for all of us," said Darius, now sounding hurt. "Your marriage to the king will hopefully bring peace between Zachavi and Lakishea."

"That's what it is? I'm a peace treaty? You're just going to trade me off just so our two countries will get along better? Don't you even care about me and my happiness?" Ranaya choked on the tears that were threatening to fall.

"Ranaya, sometimes being a royal means you have to sacrifice your personal happiness for the good of your kingdom. Things don't always go our way, and we have to accept that. I'm sorry, but that is what is happening to you."

Darius offered her a small smile. "Besides, that's how I met your mother. We, too, had an arranged marriage."

Ranaya had had enough for the day and was about to leave when Darius pulled her back. "Don't go yet. Listen to me."

"Maybe I don't want to be a royal," Ranaya murmured. "Sometimes I wish I was a normal peasant girl instead of a princess—or else that I was never born in the first place."

For just a moment, Darius looked ready to slap her, but then he sighed. "That kind of wishing won't change anything. It doesn't change who you are, nor your destiny." An unpleasant warning note crept into his tone. "You will marry King Karik, and you will learn to accept that fact and to stop feeling sorry for yourself."

Ranaya sighed. She just couldn't win.

*Wait until Dari hears of this,* she thought. Dari was her older brother, who at that time was out surveying the country. His real name was Darius Yarkish the Second, but everyone referred to him as Dari.

"Can I go now?" she asked, wanting to just hide in the stables and have a good cry.

"Go on. I think we've both said enough." Darius waved her away, and she couldn't help but feel like one of the king's subjects rather than his daughter.

Ranaya didn't run away like she did before. She walked this time. She trudged slowly along; barely able to hold her head up, hoping no one else would notice her.

No one was in sight as she entered the stables and headed for the far end. She opened the door to the last stall and was greeted by a friendly whicker from a beautiful black mare. The horses always seemed to be drawn to her.

"Hello, Ebony," she said, wiping her eyes as she settled into the hay next to the horse.

She allowed herself to have a good cry, knowing no one was there to see or hear—or so she thought. By the time she had finished crying, she heard someone walk in.

Thinking it was Harry, she muttered, "Harry, you know I don't like to be disturbed when I…" She stopped in surprise as she realized it was not Harry, but the new stable-hand. She jumped quickly to her feet, trying to brush the hay from her dress.

"Your Highness!" Lando looked and sounded just as surprised. "I didn't know—I'm sorry. Really, I am." He didn't hesitate to bow. He had a pitchfork in his hand that he had to juggle to keep from dropping.

"Ranaya," she corrected him. "No, I should be the one who's sorry. You didn't know I was in here." Despite herself, she had to laugh at his expression.

"Ranaya," he smiled sheepishly. "I was just going to muck out the stall."

"Here," she said, taking the pitchfork from him, much to his astonishment. "Since I'm already in here, allow me. You go get the cart."

Lando's jaw dropped. "I—I'm not supposed to let you do that," he protested when he found his voice again. "I'll likely get fired or executed for allowing the princess to do manual labor, which should only be done by sla—" Ranaya silenced him by putting her hand on his shoulder.

"Lando, everyone knows I enjoy working in the stables. You won't get fired or executed." She offered him a reassuring smile.

Lando sighed, but did as he was told and went to retrieve the cart used specially for mucking.

Ranaya had to admit, she rather liked this new stable hand. Maybe they would see each other more often. She was already putting the pitchfork to good use before he even came back with the cart. "If you would like, you could go ahead and groom Ebony," she suggested as he stood there, looking like he didn't know what to do with himself. That stall must have been his last.

He didn't waste any time getting to it.

It was all Ranaya could do to keep from laughing at his quick actions. For a moment, she almost forgot about her talk with her father and the ugly thoughts of marrying Karik.

Maybe, she thought, just maybe, she and Lando could be friends.

The Slaves of Zachavi

# Chapter 2

As soon as Ranaya had finished with the stall, she visited her special spot in the woods, where she liked to practice. No one knew she liked archery and fencing. She kept it a secret from everyone except her brother Dari, who often fenced with her when he wasn't traveling.

Dressed in her 'boy's clothes', the princess sneaked out through the trap door in her room. This special door led to a secret passage that went all the way to the back of the castle. There was no one to see her, but she didn't want to take any chances.

When she was outside, she made a dash for the dense forest, keeping her eyes peeled, ignoring the thorns that tried to snag onto her breeches. Everything was still damp from the earlier rain.

In the woods, she passed by a good number of birds and deer as she made her way to the hollow tree that contained her sword, bow, and arrows. As she nocked an arrow into place, she imagined the target secured to the old oak to be King Karik himself, which helped some with her aim.

As if out of nowhere, a dagger hissed past her, stabbing the bulls-eye.

Ranaya gasped in surprise and amazement at the perfect shot. Glancing around to see who could have executed such a shot, she half-expected to see Karik. To add to her surprise, if such a thing possible, Lando stood behind her, looking sheepish.

"That was an incredible shot!" Ranaya cried. "How did you learn to throw so well?"

"My father taught me everything I know," Lando replied with a smile as he went to retrieve his dagger.

"Your father must be an amazing man."

"Yes, he is," Lando murmured, looking around bemusedly. "You're not too bad of a shot yourself. Who taught you archery?"

"Dari, my brother. He's away right now." Ranaya felt a pang of longing at the thought of her beloved brother. "He taught me swordsmanship as well." She looked around to see what Lando was looking at, seeing nothing out of the ordinary. He was truly a strange man.

"Ah, a swords-woman? How do your parents feel of your aptitudes?" Lando had that look on his face that Ranaya was quite familiar with; it was the look many people wore when they thought they were saying more than they should.

"They know nothing about it." Ranaya felt a twist of worry. If Lando told Harry about this, Harry would tell someone else and eventually it would reach her parents... and then she would be in big trouble.

Lando smiled. "Don't worry," he reassured her. "If you don't want the others to know, I won't say a word."

She dared to breathe freely again, and she smiled at him. "Thank you."

"I should get back to work. Harry appointed me as a temporary woodcutter since my work at the stables is done." Lando fiddled with the ax tied to his belt that Ranaya had not noticed until now. "I better get to the chopping. Perhaps you and I could do a little fencing sometime."

"That would be nice," said Ranaya appreciatively. Her day was certainly turning out better than it had started. She hadn't known Lando for very long, and already he felt like a close friend to her—a friend she sincerely hoped to keep.

In the weeks that followed, Ranaya tried to make the most of the time she had with Lando, helping him adjust to the area and know where to find certain things. One day, after Lando had finished his work and was resting on a hay bale, he asked, out of the blue, "Would you like to do some fencing?"

Ranaya cocked a shrewd eyebrow at him. "Are you challenging me?" Inwardly, she was thrilled. Finally she had someone to practice with!

Rising smoothly to his feet, Lando walked to a spot where a pack and sheath were leaning against the wall. He unsheathed a very splendid-looking sword and pointed it playfully at Ranaya. She laughed. "I'll take that as a yes."

Just as Lando was putting the sword away, Harry walked in. "You had better not go anywhere yet, Your Highness," he said, "wherever you're heading. King Karik has requested your presence in the garden. He wishes to speak to you about future plans." He set down a sack he'd been carrying over his shoulder with a grunt.

Ranaya groaned. "Meet me in the forest in two hours," she whispered to Lando, leaning close to his ear.

He jerked back as if afraid to get too close. This surprised Ranaya, but she didn't let him see it and she said nothing about it.

As she begrudgingly set off for the garden, she thought, *'Future plans', indeed. Hang your 'future plans', Karik! I wouldn't marry you if you were the last man in the realm of Elwood!* She kicked out furiously at a stone, sending it skittering into a bush.

Ranaya had half-hoped Karik would not be there when she arrived. To her immense disappointment, he was already perched on a stone bench, near the large birdbath. The garden was a beautiful place, with hundreds of different flowers, and many beautiful marble statues graced the area. Birds flocked the birdbath, but flew away as Ranaya walked past.

"Hello," she said stiffly, not even bothering to address Karik as 'Your Majesty', as was proper. She seated herself on the bench, keeping herself as far from Karik as possible without falling off.

"I am glad you could make it," Karik said, sounding smooth and suave despite his devious expression. "I suppose you know the reason I'm here. You were betrothed at the time of your birth, and now that you are of age, I am to marry you soon."

"As if I hadn't heard," Ranaya grumbled under her breath.

"Well, it will be awhile until we are married," said Karik, acting as if he hadn't heard. "About a month. But your parents have consented for you to travel with me back to Zachavi next week."

Ranaya thought she would be sick on the spot. She couldn't leave her country in a week, let alone marry the racist king in a month!

Springing to her feet, not even caring if anyone heard her, she shouted, "I will not marry you! You cannot make me!"

Karik stood at her words. "You will, you miserable, ungrateful brat," he now growled in her face, having the odd semblance of an ominous wolf that had its prey cornered. "Whether you like it or not, it will happen one way or another. Face it, *Princess.*" He spat her title out like it had a bad taste.

Impulsively, Ranaya's hand struck out and slapped him squarely across the face. The crackle of skin against skin must have carried clear to the other end of the garden. Karik staggered, and Ranaya froze in mingled horror and admiration of her own daring.

When Karik recovered, he raised his own hand as if to slap her back. But instead, he grabbed the girl's chin and forced her to look him in the eye. "Very nice eyes," he murmured. "But that red hair is utterly unbecoming. What's even more unbecoming is that shade of skin. Only slaves are this tan." He shook his head in clear disgust. "What a sorry excuse for a princess you are."

"If you have only come to insult me, then I suggest you leave." It was all Ranaya could do to keep her voice steady and her temper in check. This man had a great deal of nerve to talk to her like that. What did it matter if her skin wasn't the preferred creamy white of other girls? There was no law against being fair-skinned or dark-skinned.

If looks could kill, the glare Karik gave her was murderous.

But, to his credit, he backed down.

Ranaya couldn't stay in this man's presence for another minute, and therefore she never hesitated to flee like a frightened rabbit. She ran for the forest.

Tears were already rolling down her cheeks when she got there, and she was sobbing so hard she could scarcely breathe. To her utter embarrassment, Lando was already there, sitting on a rock, studying something he held in his hands. Ranaya turned away to hide her face from him; surely he must think of her as a crying, whining, spoiled ninny of a princess.

Lando, surprised to see Ranaya, could tell she was upset about something. He didn't want to pry, but the question found its way off his tongue anyway: "Is something wrong?"

"This king" thinks he owns me," she sniffled, wiping her eyes. She still avoided eye contact with him as he joined her side.

"Yes, King Karik thinks he owns a lot of things." Lando's tone was strange.

"The wedding is only a while from now, and I have to go to Zachavi soon. I don't want to do this, Lando. I *can't* do this! I can't marry him! He's as cold, callous, and cruel as they come. He's the racist ruler of a racist country." By this time, Ranaya had stopped crying. She felt just a tiny bit better, having talked about it and gotten it off her chest. She should have mentioned the fact she was leaving in a week, but she just couldn't yet.

Lando said nothing. When she could bring herself to face him, she was surprised at his pained expression.

"Are you okay?"

His beautiful blue eyes met hers. "Can I tell you a secret?" He sounded gravely serious. "Promise you won't tell anyone? I know we've only known each other for three weeks, but I feel I can trust you."

"Yes, of course. What is it?"

Rather than say it outright, Lando parted his hair to one side, revealing his ears to her for the first time.

Ranaya gasped.

The ears tapered to prominent points, like leaves or the blades of spears.

"You're a… a

"Yes," Lando said softly, letting his hair tumble back into place. "I am an elf."

Ranaya understood.

Everything about Lando made a great deal more sense to her—his keen hearing, his incredible fighting skills, and his uncommon handsomeness. She also understood why he was so hesitant to speak to her of his heritage, or tell her just how old he was.

Icy fingers of fear seized the princess's heart. What if Karik found out Lando was an elf? He would have him put to death without a moment's notice! Ranaya had spent enough time in Karik's company in the last three weeks to know he was everything she thought he was, and worse—a callous, stone-hearted brute who cared about no one but himself, who was very blatant about his hatred for elves and how he intended to exterminate them all within a few months. It had been all Ranaya could do to maintain her composure, to keep herself from falling completely to pieces.

"What are you doing here?" she asked, trying to not let her panic show, though her voice wavered.

"I'm in hiding," said Lando, as if that should have explained it all.

"I-If Karik finds out who you are, he'll k-kill—" Ranaya couldn't finish the sentence; the thought was too horrible. Despite the short time she had spent in Lando's company, they had grown remarkably close. It was as if they'd known each other for years rather than weeks.

If anything happened to Lando, Ranaya doubted she could bear it.

"Don't go there, Ranaya." Lando placed his finger over her lips to silence her. "They haven't found out yet. There is a good chance they'll never find out. I'm only hiding until my father sends me word that we can be together again."

"Why aren't you with your family?" Ranaya asked as Lando hauled her to her feet.

"It's hard to hide when you're in a large group. Those of my family are the only ones hiding by themselves. Everyone else stayed in a hidden cavern. My father didn't think it was safe to stay with the others. We decided hiding wasn't the best choice, and that we should live in different kingdoms and act like humans."

Ranaya said no more for a time after that. She had to fight the temptation to reach out and touch one of Lando's leaf-shaped ears.

After a long silence, Lando unsheathed his sword. "Now, how about that match?" he asked, with that mischievous glint in his eye. This would mark the first time they had an official round.

The fact he could be so cheerful despite his circumstances amazed Ranaya. She shook her head and laughed as she retrieved her sword from the hollow tree.

"Oh, great shards of rocks! We don't have any armor!" Lando exclaimed, remembering how dangerous it was to fight with swords without the necessary protection.

"I have it covered," Ranaya chuckled, amused at his strange saying. It must have been some sort of invective among elves. She felt good that she could be herself around him, that he didn't need pretend he was something he was not. She returned to the hollow tree and came back bearing two breast plates. She gave Lando the one that belonged to her brother since it was larger. Hers didn't fit well, since it was made for a man, but she had to make do.

"You know, that isn't very becoming of you," Lando teased her as she slipped on her armor. He circled her, wielding his sword playfully.

"Neither is your nose," Ranaya teased back. "Rules?"

"Watch your face, make sure to avoid touching the parts of your opponent's body where there is no armor, and no going after the legs with your hilt." As they crossed their swords, he said with a grin, "I'll try to be easy on you."

Ranaya gave him a bored look. "You got me," was all she said.

She then caught him off guard, knocking her sword against his with a clang that vibrated through her whole arm, then leaping lithely away.

"A-ha!" Lando attempted to knock her sword away from her, but it almost turned out the other way around.

Before two full minutes had passed, Ranaya had Lando pinned to the ground with her sword pressed to his breast plate. Lando was impressed at the princess's skill. "And that wasn't even trying," Ranaya said matter-of-factly as she helped Lando to his feet.

"I would hate to see what you're like when you're sincerely trying."

"That was beguiling." Ranaya stripped off her armor and hid it and her sword away in the tree before anyone else would see besides Lando.

"You would think so Your Highness," he said, just to nettle her a little more.

"Do *not* call me that!" Ranaya fell for the bait. She whirled on Lando, who looked like he was having a difficult time trying to not laugh.

"Temper, temper," he tutted. "I guess it's true what they say about redheads—they are flaming hot under the collar!"

"Why, you—!" She bolted after him as he turned and made a run for it.

They both laughed; she wasn't really mad at him, and they both knew it.

All the trees rushed past them in a blur of green. The rushing breeze was crisp and wonderful. Ranaya never recalled feeling so free.

Lando, like all elves, was a swift runner. It wasn't long before he disappeared, and Ranaya found herself alone. *Elves,* she harrumphed to herself as she slowed down to catch her breath, looking around to see if he was hiding behind a tree somewhere, ready to jump out and scare her.

"Lando, where are you?" she called.

Only the silence of the forest answered her.

When Ranaya searched around a few trees, Lando was nowhere to be seen. Unable to help it, she felt her stomach twist into a knot of uneasiness. Something felt wrong. She couldn't say what it was, but there was no mistaking it.

A few minutes later, that old panic rose up again. Since Lando had told her he was an elf, she couldn't help fearing for his safety.

"Lando, please, don't scare me like this—" Her sentence was cut off when she accidentally plowed into something; she lost her balance and fell over backwards. Looking up, she saw that she had bumped into Lando. He stood with his back facing her, hardly aware of her presence. He was staring at something ahead. He was still as a tree, his shoulders tense.

"Lando, what—"

"Karik is looking for you," Lando said before she could ask the question. His strange tone frightened her.

"How do you know?" Ranaya whispered, fighting the urge to be sick. Knowing Karik, he would undoubtedly find out she was spending all of her free time with a mere stable-hand, and he would most likely threaten Lando… or hurt him.

"Look," Lando said, without altering his gaze.

She looked in the same direction, and sure enough, Karik was not far away.

"Hide!" she hissed, yanking on Lando's arm.

He willingly followed her behind the nearest big tree.

Ranaya was ashamed at her own behavior. Why did she always have to act like such a big coward? Why should she be so scared of Karik? She was hardly in fear of her own safety, except for those times when Karik looked quite ready to slap her around. After all, Karik was a big man, and he could deliver a powerful blow if he wanted to.

Lando had to admit he himself was a little puzzled at the way Ranaya was acting. Normally when there was a problem, she learned to face it dead-on; today, however, she was different. She held tightly onto his arm, her long nails cutting into him.

The crunching of leaves signaled Karik's closeness. Each crunch made Ranaya's heart beat faster; she wondered that the beating of her heart alone did not alert him to their hiding place.

"Ranaya, my dear, where are you?" Karik called out in a voice that was like poisoned honey. Ranaya had an unpleasant feeling that he knew she was behind that very tree.

As always, she acted on a whim.

Without a second thought, she snatched Lando's sword from his belt and jumped out from behind the tree, ready to fight if need be.

Lando was horrified. He had grown to care very much for Ranaya and he didn't want her to get hurt. He could perfectly defend himself.

"Ranaya, no!" he shouted, but it was already too late.

"Ah, there you are," said Karik nonchalantly, looking at the sword in her hand with disinterest. His gaze shifted to Lando, who had joined her side.

Suddenly Ranaya realized she couldn't reveal her knowledge and skill with the sword. What had she been thinking?

"Really, girl, do you think you could use that thing? Seriously." Karik shook his head at her as if she were the dumbest creature alive.

"You're right," she said, dropping the sword as if it had burned her. Lando looked at her quizzically, but bent down to retrieve the sword without a word.

"And who are you?" Karik asked Lando, not even bothering to mask his distrust and hate.

Ranaya's eyes widened as she noticed Karik had four large, deadly-looking knives attached to his belt. As if Karik had read her mind, he brandished one of those knives and advanced on them with a malicious look on his face.

Quickly pulling Ranaya behind him, Lando snapped at the Zachavian king, "You leave her out of this!"

"Why? I ought to have taught her a lesson weeks ago when she told her father she wouldn't marry me. You're not even worth marrying, you scum." To Ranaya, Karik went on, "But the thing is, your father and my father arranged the marriage, leaving neither of us any say in the matter. So now I have no choice but to marry you... unless I kill you, which is an option."

The next thing anyone knew, Karik had thrown the knife. Ranaya screamed as it hissed through the air toward them.

Suddenly, with lightning swiftness, Lando's hand shot out and caught the knife in midair. It had come dangerously close to impaling him, but he dropped it casually to the ground, his expression unchanged.

Weak with shock at what had just happened, Ranaya sank to her knees.

"My, my, how impressive you must think yourself." Karik laughed. "Let's see what you'll do when you have *three* of these things coming at you! I'll tend to you later," he warned Ranaya, who didn't answer.

Lando barely had time to think as three knives sailed out at him.

But he caught each one of them at the same time, letting them drop to the ground like the first one.

"That wasn't even trying," he said, quoting Ranaya, and it was true.

Karik spat, on the ground in disappointment and fury; before collecting his daggers and turning back, to the castle. "So help me," he vowed, jabbing all four in their direction, "if I ever see you two together again, there will be hell to pay."

"You won't get away with this," Lando yelled as Karik walked away.

Karik didn't look back, but his last words were, "If you tell anyone I just attempted to kill you, they would never believe

you. No one believes the word of a mere stable boy over that
of          a          king."

# Chapter 3

Ranaya struggled to her feet as Lando turned to her to make sure she was all right. "You saved my life," she said, managing a quivering smile. She was truly grateful, but embarrassment tangled with her gratitude, along with a touch of indignation.

"You would have done the same thing for me," Lando assured her.

She could think of no suitable reply to this. No, she thought, she couldn't do the same if their situation was reversed and he had been the one standing behind her. She wouldn't have been able to catch a dagger in midair like that—not without getting injured.

"I should have taken care of myself," she said.

Lando shook his head. "Ranaya, sometimes we have to let someone else save us. There comes a time when we simply cannot do it on our own."

Ranaya objected, but he held up a hand to silence her.

"Please, let me finish. I don't mean to show that you are weak. But Karik is a dangerous man as you may well know; he hurts and kills for the mere sport of it. He has many victims on his list. I don't intend to have you become his next victim. If you'll let me, I will help to protect you."

His eyes pleaded with her, and while part of Ranaya sought his protection, another part of her was terrified of him putting his life on the line for her sake. "No… I can't let you do that to yourself. I'm sorry." She couldn't bring herself to look at him while she said this.

Lando looked as if she had broken his heart. But he said no more on the matter and did his best to hide his emotions as they walked back to the stables. Even so he made a silent vow he would protect Ranaya, with or without her approval. He'd meant what he said when he did not intend to have her fall prey to that sorry excuse for a human.

They were both quiet as they reached the stables, both immersed in deep thought. Harry and two other men were out in the corral, replacing the shoes on the horses. Harry looked up as Lando and Ranaya came along. "There you are!" he called to Lando. "I've needed an extra hand with these horses."

Ranaya pretended to not have seen him, while Lando only said, "Yes, sir."

Ranaya stood still for another minute at the fence, debating on whether she should go inside the castle. If she did, she would most likely find herself face-to-face with Karik. Then again, if she didn't go anyway, she would be in big trouble; her parents thought it was bad enough to be in the stable an hour, let alone all day.

The butler alerted her of suppertime as she stepped through the door. She immediately felt sick to her stomach as she dashed up the stairs to her chamber. She always sat across from Karik at the table, which would only make things worse. Who could eat when there was a murderer in front of them?

Ranaya couldn't very well skip supper, either. She had lost much of her appetite since Karik came along, and it was showing. She was already skinny enough, but now she was becoming almost gaunt. At least she could get away with a loose corset, she thought as a maid helped her change her dress and fix her hair.

By the time she got to the dining room, her parents and Karik had almost finished eating. Darius and Karik both gave her an unpleasant glare that she tried to ignore as she sat down, trying to act casual, and picked at her food. Her mother, Helena, didn't look up from her plate.

Karik's gaze remained fixed on her, and almost without realizing it, she dropped her fork with a loud clank. Darius and now Helena looked at her, and after a few long, intense minutes, Darius broke the cold silence. "Do you have something to tell us?"

Glaring at Karik as she shoved her plate away, Ranaya burst out, "Yes, I do!"

Her parents looked a little startled, but Karik continued to look at her maliciously.

With a sigh, Darius asked, though he was sure he already knew the answer, "What is it?"

"Do you realize who you are marrying me to?" Ranaya cried out, her shrill voice resounding through the hall.

"Ranaya Elani Yarkish, you watch your tongue!" Helena sharply admonished.

"THIS MAN HAS THREATENED AND TRIED TO KILL ME!" Ranaya all but screamed, pointing a shaking finger at Karik, who took a quiet sip from his goblet as if nothing out of the ordinary were happening.

"SILENCE!" Darius commanded, banging his fist emphatically on the table.

In contrast to her husband, Helena said quietly but coolly, "Stop trying to make up excuses for not marrying King Karik. We all know about your affair with that new stable-hand; we should fire him on the spot."

It was now Ranaya's turn to glare murderously at Karik; the sly snake had tried to make it sound to her parents like she didn't want to marry him because she was in love with Lando and trying to cover it up by lying like a crazy woman.

"No!" Ranaya cried. "I tell you, Karik really threatened me, tried to kill—"

"Tried to kill you, did he?" Darius raised an eyebrow. "And if that's the case, how did you get away?" He spoke that last part in a rather joking matter    that made her blood boil.

"I tell you, she's making this all up," Karik said, speaking up for the first time that evening. "She's simply not right in the head…"

"The stable-hand he accuses me of being in love with saved me!" But even as she said it, Ranaya knew it was no use; Karik was winning and the only sensible thing she could think of was to just run away.

"That's a lie!" Karik hissed through his teeth.

Ranaya had had enough of this, more than enough. She pushed back her chair and stormed out of there, ignoring the others as they called out her name. Oh, how she despised her name; how she wished she had another name entirely. Maybe she could use her middle name when she ran away.

She stayed in her room well into the night. She dared not go to sleep, knowing that Karik's bedchamber was just across the hall from hers. There was no telling what he might try to do to her that night. She didn't even have a lock, had never owned once since she was a little girl, when she had been punished for not doing as she was told and locking her door on her parents. They'd had a servant remove the lock, and now she had no privacy in her own room.

If she had a weapon handy, she wouldn't have been so unnerved about the idea of Karik coming in and wringing her neck, but she didn't have anything on her.

She lay in her bed until the early hours of the morning before she bolted out of bed, deciding the stables would be a much safer place to sleep. "Bother that," she muttered as she snatched up her sheepskin blanket. She donned her robe and used the trap door behind her bookshelf that led out of the castle.

When she reached the stable doors, she did a quick check to make sure no one else was around. As soon as she shut the doors, she wished for a torch or a lantern, anything that had light. As she groped through the darkness, she froze briefly at the sight of a light glowing in the loft. If she hadn't been so exhausted, she would have gone up and investigated.

Once she reached Ebony's stall, she collapsed into the soft hay with a sigh, pulling her thick blanket over herself. She fell asleep quickly, ignoring Ebony as the mare snuffled curiously at the intruder in her stall.

*Lando stumbled through the forest, calling out Ranaya's name. He held his heart as it throbbed with pain with each step he took. He was dying, and he knew it. The pain of losing her was eating away at him until there was nothing left. (Elves feel the deepest emotions and can very well die of sorrow.)*

*She never said goodbye. She just ran away, and no one could find a trace of her. Lando had been cleaning out the stables day after day, until he was too weak and now he wanted to make that last attempt to find her, in spite of his failing heart. If she only came back, maybe his health would turn around.*

*He used to think he loved her as a best friend, but now he knew such wasn't the case. He was in love with her. Why else would her absence have such an effect on him? Why     else was he dying?*

*Some twigs snapped behind him, but Lando paid no attention as he staggered deeper into the forest. All he wanted was to see his princess, if for one last time, and tell her how he felt. Suddenly, he stopped at the feel of a blade against his back.*

*"You don't look so well, boy," said a voice as cold as the steel of the sword.*

*Turning, Lando found himself face-to-face with Karik.*

*Without warning, Karik seized Lando by the hair and yanked his head back with almost enough force to break his neck. Lando cried out in sharp pain as Karik leaned over him with a very smug look on his face; Karik stood a few inches taller than Lando. (This was odd; Lando was a good 5 inches than Karik....)*

*"I've been studying you since the day Ranaya left," he said. "I've noticed how your health has taken a nosedive. I know you're trying to hide it—but I know what you are." Karik lifted the hair covering Lando's ears, revealing the prominent points he had tried to hide for so long. "You cockroaches are so hard to get rid of." Karik let go of a handful of blonde hair but kept his sword pointed at his foe.*

*Lando made no response, knowing he was in no condition to fight.*

*"From what I gather, there are three ways to kill an elf—fire, steel, and, I dare say, a broken heart." Karik's eyes brightened. "Ranaya has already taken the advantage of killing you," he said, all but gleefully. He laughed as the sword lowered further.*

*That last remark made Lando furious enough to not care how weak he was as he launched at the accursed Zachavian King. How dare he use Ranaya's name and the word "killing" in the same sentence!*

43

*In less time than it takes to blink, the sword pierced Lando directly in the heart.*

*Only a second later, the elf dropped down dead.*

Ranaya's own scream woke her up. Gasping for breath, cold perspiration running down her face in steady streams, she took a minute to recognize her surroundings. Even with her eyes fully open, the nightmare she'd just had still lingered in her mind. She had left Lando, and he had died because of her. Even if it was only a dream, it all seemed so real; what was worse, she felt everything Lando felt. It was as if she were looking through his eyes, feeling through his heart— and it terrified her.

Ranaya felt the desperate urge to see him now, to know for herself that he was alive. She knew she couldn't leave him now! She wouldn't even think it.

The girl began to cry though she tried her best to muffle the noise. Her heart pounding, a mile a second in fear, she looked around and found a light coming from the hall. She shrank back against the wall as the occupant of that light opened the stall door. Her eyes widened at the sight.

Instead of Karik with a lantern, as she had expected, it was Lando; what was even more surprising was that the light was coming off of *him*.

Ebony snorted in surprise and craned her neck to stare at the elf.

Ranaya knew elves were extraordinary beings, but she had no idea they glowed in the dark. All she could do was sit there and stare.

"Ranaya! What are you doing in here?" Lando looked just as surprised to see her as she was to see him.

Ranaya couldn't speak. Her astonishment was too great, and she feared she would cry again, out of pure relief.

"Ranaya, what's wrong? Has he hurt you? If he hurt you, I'm going to—" Lando trailed off as he knelt beside her in the straw, looking into her face. She was not hurt, but it was clear from a glance she'd had a dreadful scare.

Closing her eyes, Ranaya said weakly, "I... it's nothing. Just a bad dream, nothing more." A warm wave of relief swept through her, washing away her astonishment and fear.

"Do you mind telling me about it?" she heard him ask, his concern evident in his voice.

"Y-you... you were dying... K-Karik..." Ranaya broke off with a sob, feeling humiliated for acting like such a weak woman in front of him.

She felt Lando draw her closer and envelop her in a hug. "Shhh," he soothed. "Don't cry, Ranaya. It's all right. Surely, it couldn't have been that bad."

"But it was, Lando. You were already dying, and he killed you. I-it was so real…" Ranaya fought to get hold of herself.

"Do I look dead to you?" he asked, attempting gentle humor.

She could only sniffle in reply. She tried to pull back from him, but found she couldn't move; some strange spell seemed to hold her in place. "No… but you're glowing," she mused, looking up into his face.

Lando made a strange expression. "Unfortunately, I never do stop glowing. You just can't see it in the daylight. It's an elf trait that may one day betray me."

Almost without realizing it, Ranaya touched his cheek. Surprised at her own daring, she dropped her hand again; she had never touched any part of his body, other than his hand. "I'm sorry," she said. "I'm sorry I got all emotional on you."

"Everybody gets emotional sometimes," Lando said, trying to hide his shock at her spontaneous sign of affection. "It's perfectly natural."

Ranaya yawned. She wanted to snuggle back into his arms, but knew better than that. She would probably make his heart fail him altogether.

"I guess I better let you return to sleep." Lando got up, and then stopped to ask, "What are you sleeping in here for, anyway?"

"Because it's more peaceful in here... and I feel safer," Ranaya couldn't help confessing.

Lando frowned. "Don't let Karik get to you. Just because he's a king, he thinks he owns everyone and has the right to manipulate them in any way he chooses."

Ranaya wrapped herself more snugly in her sheepskin blanket. She doubted she could ever get back to sleep, but she tried to not let Lando know. The light radiating from his body was strangely comforting, even as fear that he would leave her pierced her heart. "I know," the girl sighed, feeling small and almost childlike beneath his gaze.

"I should go," Lando said as he rose to his feet.

"No," Ranaya found herself blurting out. "Don't go." Her own fear surprised her and embarrassed her. What was the matter with her? She'd never felt the need for anyone to look after her, to protect her from harm.

Lando looked down at her with grave concern. It wasn't like her to be this way. The next thing Ranaya knew, Lando's arms enfolded her once more, making her feel more safe and secure than she had ever felt in her life. At length, he sang to her in a foreign language, most likely his own. It was the most beautiful sound she had ever heard; it was enough to bring new tears to her eyes. She had heard stories of elves seducing humans with their singing, which lead to deadly results... but this was different.

This was a lullaby, and a love song, all rolled into one, and sung in the voice of an angel:

"Sleep now, my dear one,
While the moon keeps guard in the sky.
Rest now, my sweet one,
While the stars watch from on high.
A soft lullaby sounds from the stream,
And I shall be with you when you dream."

Already, Ranaya's eyelids were drooping, and her head lolled against Lando's chest. All traces of fear left her, and waves of sweet peace flooded through her. By the time Lando was finished, Ranaya was sleeping soundly.

With some reluctance, he laid her down on the soft bed of hay, making sure the blanket covered her well.

Then he arose to his feet and with one final glance, closed the door to Ebony's stall.

Ranaya awoke to a bad crick in her neck and a noisy shout coming from the stable doors. "Ranaya, where are you? If your father finds out you've been sleeping in the stables, he will have your head on a silver platter! Not to mention mine!"

It was Gertrude, Ranaya's lady's maid. Naturally, she would have been the first to discover Ranaya was not in her bedchamber.

Ranaya groaned and sat up, shaking hay from her hair. It was still dark outside, and that annoyed her very much. Her head spun as she stood up. "Coming."

Rustling sounded in the loft and Ranaya flinched. Lando was getting a rude awakening from Gertrude's yelling.

"Very well," Gertrude sniffed in her devil-may-care way.

Ranaya had always longed for another maid, but she had been stuck with Gertrude since the day of her birth. If only the woman could be a little less uptight—or at the least, not own a voice that could rouse the dead.

Ranaya was just about to head for the door when she heard a, "Psst!" Her gaze lifted to the loft, from which it came.

Sure enough, Lando was awake and looking down at her. His light cast the hay and wood around him in a strange but beautiful shade of blue. The sight was quite dazzling, and Ranaya had to force herself to concentrate on what he was saying.

"After work is done, meet me at our place," he told her in a voice loud enough for her, but too soft for Gertrude to catch. His blue eyes twinkled with an uncharacteristic mischief.

Thoughts of the previous night came flooding back to her: the beautiful song, his beautiful voice; she had fought back tears when she heard him. Even now, the memory of the music made her knees weak.

Ranaya nodded with a smile and made the dreaded procession to the castle, knowing too well from experience the dangers of Darius's wrath.

Much to her dismay and disgust, Karik stood in the hall, blocking her way. She plastered a fake smile to her face when she came up to him though inwardly she simmered.

"Looking forward to spending the day with me, my dear?" Karik asked in a voice made of equal parts of sugar and venom.

It took almost everything Ranaya possessed just to hold back her tongue. Knowing the consequences if she refused him, she gave a curt nod and pushed past him.

Once inside her bedchamber, she flung herself onto her bed, she muttered, "In your dreams."

"Your Highness?" A frantic maid shook Ranaya awake.

With a groan, Ranaya tried to pull her coverlet over her head. "What is it, Gertrude?"

"You've overslept, and His Majesty is waiting for you in the gardens," Gertrude said, pulling the coverlet away from the protesting princess. "I was to summon you and dress you at once."

Ranaya sat up, rubbing at her eyes. "Oh, very well."

Without a pause, Gertrude began the rummage through the countless dresses that Ranaya despised, all frilly and lacy with ridiculous beading. After what seemed like forever, she settled on a turquoise dress with beads, generous sleeves, and a gown about as big as the realm of Elwood itself.

Thus began the usual, tedious task of layering the undergarments, including the wire cage that went over Ranaya's hips, the dreaded corset, the awful stockings that itched like anything, and then the slippers with the heels that made Ranaya feel as though she were constantly walking on her tiptoes. By the time Gertrude was done, Ranaya's feet were already aching and she could barely draw breath.

Normally she would have done without the crown, but today she was forced to wear it.

All this fuss…just to impress a king, who was about the sorriest excuse for a king imaginable.

By the time Ranaya grudgingly made her way to the gardens, Karik was standing by the birdbath. From the corner of her eye, Ranaya noticed Lando out by the stables, doing his daily grooming of the horses. Oh, what she wouldn't have given to be there beside him right about now.

"Ready for our little stroll?" Karik asked, holding out his arm.

Trying to keep a straight face, she took it and he led her off.

"I thought we'd go through the maze your father constructed not too long ago. What do you say?" Karik's smile and tone were pleasant enough, but his eyes warned Ranaya that there would be hell to pay if she did not accept.

Ranaya struggled to swallow the rocklike lump in her throat. How she wished Lando was there, but if Karik found out he was an elf, he would execute him faster than blinking. Just the thought of losing him, her best and only true friend, made Ranaya shiver, despite the rising heat of the day.

Her thoughts were lost as Karik yanked her into the maze. She had never tried the crazy, winding pathways before, but she was determined to lose Karik as soon as possible.

Karik continued to pull her along through the maze until they were somewhere in the middle before he stopped. Ranaya knew from the glint in his eye he was up to something. She tensed, feeling like a deer ready to flee from the hunter.

And then he did do something. He grabbed Ranaya and nearly crushed her against him. She cried out and struggled to get free, but his grip was like a vise. Then his mouth was over hers, kissing her to the point of smothering.

It was the most disgusting thing she had ever endured, and she slapped him across the face and somehow found the strength to break loose.

Karik snarled and yanked her back, earning a sharp bite that made him yelp.

"You little viper!" Karik snarled.

Trying not to trip over her many skirts, Ranaya ran the opposite direction as fast as she could, winding her way through the maze, and praying to God that she would find the end. Everywhere she turned, all she could see was green, and more green, and the multiple twists and turns made her dizzy.

Just when she thought she'd never get out of there, she tripped over something and fell. The next thing she knew, she was on the ground, her head resting on something that turned out to be a boot. Looking up, Lando's stunned face greeted her.

"Are you all right? Why were you running so fast? You acted like a ghost was after you!" Bending, Lando clasped her hand in his and pulled her to her feet.

Ranaya shook her head, barely having the breath to say, "I don't want to talk about it."

Even so Lando could guess. "Karik again?"

She nodded and bit her lip.

"Meet me later in the woods?" he gently asked.

"A-all right." Ranaya's voice cracked as she pulled away. With one last look at the elf, she bolted for the castle to change her dress.

# Chapter 4

Ranaya stripped herself of her royal gown and replaced it with something much more comfortable, more peasant-like. Then she made her break for the woods, wanting to get as far away from that place before Karik found his way out of the maze, knowing how livid he was bound to be.

So intent was she in her escape she hardly paid attention to where she was going and soon ran smack into what she at first thought was a tree.

That tree turned out to be Lando, and the force with which they collided was such that they both ended up on the ground, with Ranaya on top.

Her green eyes met his blue ones. She could make out every detail of his face, from his high forehead and angular cheekbones, to his well-sculpted nose and lips. He was, beyond a doubt, the most beautiful creature she had ever thought to exist.

Ranaya gasped, realizing how close they were, and quickly rolled off, blushing. Never in her life had she felt so embarrassed. What was she thinking? How could she even harbor such a thought?

She turned away, feeling his intent gaze upon her nonetheless, and her heart raced.

Lando looked at the princess for but a moment before getting up and pulling her to her feet. She had to lean against his chest to keep from falling, but he only laughed. A sound as sweet as birdsong. "Come with me," he said, slipping his hand into hers. "I want to show you a special place I have found. Don't worry, it's not far."

Puzzled, yet gratified, Ranaya let him lead the way.

They came to a laughing stream. A crystal waterfall spilled over the sun-kissed rocks into a small pool as blue and clear as the summer sky. To Ranaya's astonishment, Lando pulled off his cloak and tunic and tossed them into a nearby bush.

"Lando, what are you *doing?*"

Her only answer was a cheeky grin before he made a swan-like dive into the pool. Ranaya gasped as he shot through the surface and splashed her before diving back under. From the way he took to the water, one would think he had gills and a tail, if they knew none better.

"Lando?" Ranaya called, taking a tentative step closer to the rock-dotted edge and gazing into the water for any sign of the elf. Then two white, strong hands seized her feet, pulling her into the water before she had time to catch her breath, let alone scream.

Unfortunately for Ranaya, she couldn't swim well, so the moment she landed in the water, she panicked. She tried to scream for Lando as he swam away, but her open mouth only allowed access to the water. She fought desperately to stay afloat, but the more she struggled, the farther she sank.

Her lungs burned from the lack of air, and a strange, rather fuzzy blackness clouded her vision.

Just when she was on the brink of drowning, strong arms caught her round the waist and pulled her up. She was vaguely aware of Lando as he dragged her onto the bank.

Lando's heart skipped a beat as he realized the girl wasn't breathing. Giving no thought to the later consequences, he snatched his dagger and cut a slit in Ranaya's dress to reach that death contraption she wore that stifled her breathing even in harmless situations.

The strings that held the thing together proved too complicated to untie by hand, so Lando just cut them as well (it was almost all he could do to keep a steady hand), and then used his bare hands to rip the whalebone cage open.

With a violent jerk, Ranaya coughed up abundant amounts of water. She could only draw in a few ragged breaths at a time, feeling she would never breathe properly again. It was after she had settled down she became aware of her open dress and corset; only her chemise remained intact.

"I'm sorry about that," Lando said, turning a rather unbecoming shade of red.

"You did what you had to." Ranaya's voice sounded strange to her own ears. She was inexpressibly thankful to

Lando, but embarrassment tangled with her gratitude. Why couldn't she have learned to swim before now? Of all the things Dari taught her, why didn't he include swimming in his lessons?

Without another word, Lando stood up and fetched his cloak to wrap around Ranaya, preserving modesty besides warmth.

"Thank you," Ranaya mumbled, pulling the cloth tighter around her shoulders. The cloth smelled like the wood, the scents sharp but also oddly soothing.

"First thing tomorrow," Lando said, "I'm teaching you how to swim."

Ranaya's jaw dropped. "What—"

Lando smiled, a spark of mischief in his blue eyes, but he said nothing as he held out his hand to her. Ranaya took it, feeling a little timid, though she hardly knew why. Her fingers tingled within his.

Could she be? No, she couldn't be! She couldn't possibly be in—she couldn't even bring herself to think the word. A fiery blush swept across her face, and she hoped Lando would think it was just the afternoon heat. Her heart resumed its crazy beating; she was sure Lando must hear it.

Suddenly Lando became as still as a statue. A strange look came over his face as he looked toward a group of trees.

"What's the—" Ranaya began, but was cut short as Lando whisked her behind a clump of bushes. She would have cried out in surprise, except he covered her mouth before she could make a sound.

"Shh!" Lando hissed into her ear. "It's Karik!"

Ranaya's blood ran cold. Karik must have been after her, all this time. From her position on the ground, she could see no trace of the man, but she had learned by now to trust Lando's judgment—and his keen sense of sight and sound.

It turned out Lando wasn't fooled, for within a few minutes, Karik emerged into view, sword in hand. Ranaya huddled closer to Lando, wishing she had brought her sword. Lando didn't have any weapons on her, either, so it would be a sorry situation indeed if Karik found them. As Karik's boots came and stood before them, Ranaya shut her eyes tightly, and Lando's arms squeezed her every bit as tightly, if not more.

"Ranaya!" Karik bellowed. "I know you're out here. You must return to the castle at once if you know what's good for you! Your whole kingdom is going under surveillance. There have been reported sightings of elves, particularly one by the name of Landrian. I mean to take him, dead or alive. His family has been plotting war against us for generations."

Ranaya shivered while Lando had gone rock-rigid.

Lakishea, Ranaya thought, undergoing an elf-hunt? Her father never said anything about elves; surely this must be Karik's doing.

When Karik was gone at last, that was when Lando released his hold. When Ranaya looked at him, his pained expression almost stopped her heart. "Lando?" she whispered. "Are you..."

"I am Landrian." The words emerged so softly that Ranaya could barely hear them, but a choked cry found its way out of her throat nonetheless.

As the two rose to their knees, Ranaya kept a fierce grip on her friend, as if he would slip away if she let him go for a second. "No," she gasped, fighting in vain to keep back tears.

Lando bowed his head, but said nothing.

"Oh, please, no," Ranaya now sobbed, feeling as if her whole world were crumbling.

Karik meant to hunt Lando, to torture him, to kill him. Did he truly know who Lando was, or was the man just clueless?

As Ranaya wept, Lando pulled her closer and enveloped her in his arms. "Shhh," he whispered in his best attempt to console her. "Shhh... don't cry."

"No! No, he can't do this! I won't have it! I won't let him!"

"Ranaya..."

Shaking her head, the girl said fiercely, "We must think of some way to get you out of this! Maybe we could make you appear more human. Maybe—" The rest of her words were cut off when Lando's lips joined hers.

What happened next, Ranaya hardly knew. She couldn't breathe, couldn't think, and could barely even see straight. As if with their own will, her hands crept up to brush through his light hair and stroke his pointed elven ears; Lando made the smallest shiver at the contact.

When the kiss broke, Lando was the first to speak. "Ranaya... I don't know how to tell you this, so I'm giving it to you straight."

Ranaya caught her breath, knowing what he was about to say, yet not daring to believe it, and yet wanting with all her aching heart to hear it.

"I love you." A bittersweet smile played on his lips, and he pressed his forehead against hers.

Ranaya's tears flowed afresh, but this time for another reason altogether.

Here he was, her best friend, proclaiming his love to the woman engaged to the man who sought his life. And yet...

As Lando's thumb brushed a tear from her cheek, she could hold back no longer.

"I love you, too... Landrian."

Lando's eyes shot up in surprise at the use of his elven name. "You're not mad that    I never told you?"

Ranaya shook her head, her finger still tracing the point of one of his ears. Then she had an idea.

"Lando—Landrian? How would you like to have rounded human ears?" She grinned through her tears.

He cocked his head in question.

Knowing they had little time to spare, Ranaya quickly stood up and laced her fingers in the elf's as he copied her movements.

She pulled him 'back to their spot'; where her tree was. She had remembered from last year. Dari had been playing around with a clay-like substance. Yet it wasn't clay. It had a realistic texture of skin and was stretchy. The putty clay-like substance was called Harisc. It only got the realistic texture when melted in hot temperatures. Dari had jokingly made two pointed ears, painted them, and placed them over Ranaya's ears, making ear holes so she could hear. The mold fit perfectly. Maybe she could take those same ears and smooth the points off? It was worth a try. She even remembered where she stored them. She had always been curious of what it would be like to be an elf. She couldn't bear to part with them. But now they had a better use.

Lando stood at the door to the tree as Ranaya hastily grabbed the box the ears were in. She frowned as she pulled them out. Wanting one more time to wear them a few seconds she slipped them over her ears. She smiled as she felt the point. It wasn't exactly like Lando's but mighty close.

She walked out just to see what Lando would do when he saw her ears.

Lando blinked in surprise then rubbed eyes and stared again. His mouth dropped open, and he reached out to touch the fake ears.

Ranaya laughed and took them off before getting her knife from its sheath. She sawed across the point until it was smooth and round.

She frowned when she realized the color was off. Her skin was a lot darker than Lando's.

She was lucky Dari loved to paint. She went back and came back out of the tree holding a tube and brush. She squirted the paint onto the brush. Biting her lip, Ranaya held the brush up to examine the color differences.

Lando stood stock-still, only his eyes moved, he stooped a little so Ranaya could reach his face.

The paint was the right shade. She brushed the paint lightly over the ears until the ears were lightened.

Ranaya smiled in triumph. Karik wouldn't be able to tell the difference. She waved them around in the air until they dried.

Lando's eyes were wide as the princess neared him to try the new ears on him. He stooped again and squeezed his eyes shut in anticipation.

She smiled as she moved his hair away.

Lando shivered from the tickling sensation as she slipped the first ear on. It was oddly uncomfortable since the new ear made his pointed one bend at the tip. It covered up his secret.

Ranaya stepped back to examine the new Lando.

Again, Lando stood still as a statue, his eyes following every movement she made. He was feeling edgy about this ordeal.

"Relax, you look like a trapped rabbit," Ranaya tried placing a hand on his shoulder, but it only reached the lower part of his chest. She settled for it since she couldn't reach his shoulders. He was so much taller than she.

Lando exhaled, realizing he had been holding his breath for a while. He forced a smile. "I'm only worried about what will happen."

"I guarantee you that Karik will be fooled and anyone else who examines you." Ranaya assured gently. Truth be told… She was just as worried but knew that they could trick everyone with these false ears. They were too realistic.

A horn sounded, signaling the kingdom the surveillance was beginning.

Ranaya and Lando both jumped in slight alarm.

She remembered the state of the dress she was wearing and panicked. She couldn't go back to the castle looking like this.

It was imaginable of what she looked like she had been doing and she couldn't have anyone think such things about her.

"My dress," Ranaya gasped, wishing she had somehow stored some extra dresses in the tree's trunk.

"There's no time," Lando grasped her hand and pulled her after him.

Ranaya pulled Lando's cloak closer around herself to hide the torn parts of her dress.

He stopped when they were at the edge of the wood.

"It's best we go our separate ways from here." Lando explained, slowly letting go of her hand. He hesitated beside her as if he didn't want to leave her.

Ranaya felt tears prick her eyes as Lando's eyes painfully searched hers. She knew what he was thinking.

"If I don't ever see you again--" he began. His eyes were becoming misty

"We will see each other again," Ranaya said stubbornly.

A smile graced Lando's features, and he wrapped his arms around her waist.

Ranaya clung to him. She would believe Lando would not be found out even if her mind was in turmoil.

"Who would have thought, a human and an elf would ever fall for each other," she whispered so softly it was more of a breath passing her lips. Even then she knew Lando heard her, for he drew her even closer.

"Who knew," he whispered back before kissing her. It was so bittersweet, Ranaya cried. No matter how much she fought it. Lando had the power to unravel her. Why did she have to be so weak in his presence?

"Just let it go, Ranaya. Let it go." Lando gave her permission to let her loose her fear and heartbreak.

"Lando," she choked, her fingers gripping his arms. She couldn't keep avoiding it. She had to tell him about leaving for Zachavi before someone else did.

"What ever is it?" His glassy blue eyes were clouded in worry.

"He's taking me away. I'm being forced to marry him. Lando, I'm leaving in a few days," Ranaya gushed.

Lando took a sharp step away from her. He looked as if he had been slapped across the face. "You didn't tell me." His voice was painfully flat.

He knew already that she was being pressured into marrying the Zachavian King but he hadn't known they were sending her away so quickly.

"Lando, I--" Ranaya stepped toward him but he looked away.

"No, you should have told me." Lando said curtly.

"I was going to."

"You let me kiss you, Ranaya."

"Because I love you," Ranaya grabbed his arm which he yanked away.

"And you're going to leave me." He looked toward her. For the first time she had known him, he looked intimidating, and she was almost afraid of him.

"I don't want to, but I have to." Ranaya stared at him.

Lando looked like he would say something, but then the horns sounded. Without another glance he was gone.

"Forward!" a guard shouted, making Ranaya jump in surprise. She had been staring at Lando, who was at the back of the line.

So far the guards had found no elves, but subject was to change.

She couldn't believe her father was actually letting this happen! Never before had he cared if he had humans and elves mixing.

Ranaya pulled Lando's cloak closer to herself as Karik glanced toward her with a sickening smile and then turning back to continue his examination over the people before him.

Lando wouldn't look at her and looked straight ahead right through her; his face was void of any expression.

She felt as if her heart was being ripped into pieces. She couldn't stand the fact she had hurt him. Why did they claim their love for each other just so it could be shattered?

Her thoughts were quickly snapped back to present as Karik shouted, yanking a woman's light hair to expose those familiar pointed ears.

Ranaya felt sick to her stomach as Karik drew a dagger.

The elf maiden's green eyes were wide as she stared at Karik. She eyed the dagger with terror.

"What is your name, elf?" Karik snarled in hatred, grabbing her by the ear roughly.

She gasped in pain, "Hadisa," squeezing her eyes shut, expecting what would happen next.

Ranaya covered her mouth in horror, trying to suppress her cry as Karik raised the dagger and slashed the elf's hair at the nape of her neck.

Hadisa cried but stood still.

"No more deceiving. You will be shamed, never able to cover your identity." Karik raised the dagger close to her heart.

A scream passed Ranaya's lips.

Karik was a monster. How could Darius even think of marrying her to him?

Lando's eyes shot to Ranaya's. They were filled with agony.

"Enough!" King Darius shouted. "You may use this treatment in Zachavi but I will not tolerate, seeing my citizens being murdered in my kingdom. Isn't cutting their hair enough?"

Karik glowered at Hadisa, but lowered his dagger. "Very well." He pushed her away, and she took a run for it.

The next few minutes were a repeat. Every few humans Karik found an elf and mercilessly slashed their hair off.

And then it was Lando's turn.

Ranaya held her breath as Karik yanked his hair away from his ears.

Lando kept his face emotionless and only glanced at Ranaya a few seconds.

Karik narrowed his eyes, but dismissed him and went on to the next person in line.

Ranaya sighed in relief as Lando passed her. His eyes were filled with pain and his hand clutched his heart as if he were hurting. Their eyes met and Ranaya felt grief fill her. The way he was looking at her was all her fault.

Ranaya lay in the bed that night. She couldn't sleep no matter what she did. Guilt was eating her up inside. She should have told Lando she was leaving before they had kissed---before he had declared his love for her and her to him.

She held the cloak he had let her borrow. Unable to put it down, its smell helped to calm her down. It smelled just like its owner. She knew she needed to give it back to him, but she was dreading confronting him.

Ranaya sighed and stared at the wooden door. She had to get up and carry Lando's cloak back. He had to need it, especially since he glowed when it was dark.

She got up to grab her robe and fastened it after lighting a candle. She quickly rolled up the cloak and tucked it under her arm.

She slowly tiptoed into the trap door of her room; sliding the bookcase open and back. The candle lit her pathway down the stairs until she met the end and was out of the castle in one leap.

# Chapter 5

Lando went straight up to his loft as soon as his examination was over. He couldn't believe Ranaya had let him proclaim his love to her and even let him kiss her. When she had known she was leaving him. It was a cruel trick to play.

Just thinking of Ranaya brought a sharp pain in Lando's chest. The pain had started not long after he had got in line to be examined.

It gradually got sharper and sharper until it made Lando bend over double with agony. It was all he could do not to cry out.

He had heard of these things, but never believed it could happen to him. The pains told him otherwise. He was dying, he could feel it. And it was all because he fell in love with someone he shouldn't.

He was warned before he set out to live among the humans by his father Landrial. Who had warned Lando that if he had ever fallen in love with a human he should expect consequences, pain, and death. He didn't think he was talking about princesses, only peasants. Being in love with a princess had to be a lot worse.

Lando knew he was doomed either way. Ranaya truly loving him or not, he would still be heartbroken when she left and would most likely die. At least if she loved him as much as he loved her, he could die a happy elf.

He should have known better than think a princess could love someone like him. He wasn't a prince or even a human just plain Landrian. Sure he had done raids in Zachavi; even helped some of his fellow elves who were enslaved escape their masters. He was considered one of the greatest warriors among his people, but a Prince no. His cousin held that title.

Lando frowned as it became dark in the barn, therefore he glowed. He yanked the fake ears from his pointed ones and placed them on a trunk beside his bed of hay. He wrapped a blanket around himself and tried to will the pain to go away from his chest. He wished for his cloak which Ranaya still had.

It was then he heard the stable doors creak upon and shut and saw a candle. A familiar face peered up into the loft.

Ranaya could see Lando's illuminated shadow as she climbed the ladder to the loft. He was sitting in the hay with his face turned away from her. He held a blanket close to himself as if trying to block the glow coming off his skin.

"I brought you your cloak," she said, sitting down on her knees beside Lando. The candle flickered wildly as she placed it on the ground beside her.

He looked toward her before looking down. "Thank you, Your Highness."

Ranaya's mouth opened in shock at his words as she placed the cloak beside him. He had never used formal names with her. She had always been Ranaya to him and nothing else since they had become friends. It stung her.

Lando grabbed the fake ears beside him and handed them to her, "I believe these are yours."

Ranaya shook her head. "You keep them, just in case you need them again." She curled his fingers around them. The contact made Lando look her in the eyes.

She let go quickly as if his glowing skin electrocuted her. "I—I'm sorry I upset you. I wanted to tell you last night as soon as I found out. I just couldn't bring myself to do it to you. I knew it would hurt you." She looked down. She couldn't take the way he was staring at her. It was like he was staring right into her soul.

"It was going to hurt me either way," Lando stated in an injured tone. He no longer sounded angry. It seemed as though he were merely stating a fact.

Ranaya looked back up, caught in his gaze again. His glassy blue eyes held hers. The barrier keeping Ranaya's feelings at bay was slowly falling to pieces and she wasn't afraid of him seeing her weaker side. He had already seen it earlier that day. She had nothing to hide from him anymore.

"I shouldn't have gotten so upset. I knew it was coming—just not this soon." Lando took her hand and placed it against his cheek. "I'm sorry. If only I could stop him."

"There's nothing you can do."

"Yes, there is, I could--" Lando started.

"And get yourself found out for what you truly are?" the thought horrified Ranaya. No way was Karik going to find out who he was. She wouldn't allow it.

Half of Ranaya wanted to jump to defense and protect Lando with her life from Karik, and then the other half was so terrified that she wished to hide behind the protection of Lando. The first half dominated the second half.

Lando didn't reply and changed the subject. "Are we back the way we were before?" A smile was visible in his eyes.

"How far back before?" Ranaya asked, feeling hopeful. She wanted to scold herself for secretly wishing they could be anything more than friends. She was engaged for goodness sake. About to be sent off to another kingdom to marry the most horrid king. She shouldn't wish for things that would end in heartbreak.

Lando seemed to know what she meant. He took both of her hands in his. "I want to spend as much time with you as possible. I don't want to regret anything. I know we only have a few days but I love you with all my heart and I--" Lando paused not knowing what else to say.

Ranaya smiled and stroked his cheek, "I don't want to waste any precious time wondering what it would have been like. We're still together. I'm not gone yet."

He smiled before bending slightly to kiss her. It was bittersweet, but it was wonderful.

Ranaya finally felt relaxed and almost safe; the first time in a while.

The stable doors creaked open and Ranaya saw Karik's form.

She gasped and grabbed Lando's cloak, throwing it over them

"The candle," Lando whispered fiercely, trying to keep his skin covered.

Ranaya without even thinking what she was doing, doused the small flickering flame with her bare hand. It was too late to uncover herself to blow it out.

Hot searing pain prickled her fingers as she bit her lip to keep from crying out. She withdrew her hand back under the cloak and cradled it against her chest.

Lando laid still, but he stared at Ranaya's hand.

"Ranaya, are you in here?" Karik's venomous, sugar coated voice rung through the stable and bounced off the walls.

Ranaya shivered. What did he want?

She heard him walk towards the ladder to the loft and stop, retreating back to the stable doors.

Knowing Karik was gone, Lando threw the cloak to the side and grabbed Ranaya's injured hand to examine the burn.

It wasn't a bad burn, but it still stung.

"Lando, it's fine," Ranaya pulled her hand away. "Really," She smiled, but it turned into a frown as it throbbed.

"You're hurt, let me help you." Lando protested, turning to unlatch the trunk that was behind them. He rummaged through his things before pulling out a small tin container and some cloth.

Ranaya watched him as he opened the lid to the container to extract a green paste-like substance. Lando took her hand and rubbed the salve onto her hand gently, then wrapped the cloth around her hand.

"There," Lando said, placing the container back into the trunk. "That should help it heal."

"What is it?" Ranaya asked, examining her hand. Whatever it was, it cooled her hand off at once.

"A homemade mixture made of different herbs." He explained before wrapping her in his cloak.

Ranaya smiled. Elves liked to use natural things.

She didn't want to go back into the castle. She was afraid of what Karik wanted. She only wished to stay right where she was at. She knew it was a disgrace for a woman to sleep beside a man—or elf even if they were doing nothing but sleeping. At this moment, she couldn't care less.

She shivered at the thought of Karik finding out, but then Lando wrapped his arms around her, and began to sing softly, and all her fear evaporated until she fell asleep.

Ranaya opened her eyes groggily, not knowing where she was. Her head laid on something solid and it was not a pillow. Her eyes rested on the navy cloak over her body... not her blanket.

Her eyes landed on the window above her. Light was streaming through it. And this was not her room.

In fact her head was laid upon Lando's shoulder. She nearly jumped out of her skin, realizing this. She had fallen asleep before she could ever go back to the castle last night. Lando had sung to her—that was when she had fallen asleep.

She had never been this close to Lando before and the nearness was almost frightening in a way.

Ranaya raised her eyes to see if he was asleep or not and gasped. Lando was staring down at her with a strange look. He almost looked sad. His expression though, changed at sign of her waking.

Ranaya shivered and wrapped the cloak closer to herself. It was always chilly in the Lakishean morning air. The thought of snuggling against Lando to keep warm was tempting, but knowing she would be in horrible trouble if she didn't hurry and get back into the castle was keeping her from the thought.

"You're finally awake," Lando teased. A smile played on his lips, but it never reached his eyes.

Ranaya knew there had to be something wrong. She pushed him gently with a small smile.

"You fell asleep on me," Lando said as Ranaya rose up into a sitting position.

"You were singing." Ranaya mused, staring at him.

Lando looked away as if ashamed of himself. "Yes, I'm sorry I did that to you. It was just that--"

Ranaya waited for him to finish but he didn't. "Just that what?" she pressed. His facial expression was worrying her. Why should he be sorry for singing to her?

"I didn't want you to go back because I didn't want you to have to face Karik. I thought the best choice was for me to put you to sleep." Lando stared down at his hands.

"You were only trying to protect me." Ranaya sighed. She didn't want Lando worrying so much about her safety. She could protect herself... even if sometimes all she wanted to do was to run somewhere and hide. Ever since Karik came along she didn't feel as fearless as she used to.

"But I should have told you what I was doing instead of tricking you like I did. It was wrong of me. I could get us both in trouble for my actions." Lando slowly stood up.

Ranaya followed suit before grabbing onto his arm.

Lando warily glanced at her.

"Even if we do get in trouble, I want you to know. I'm glad you did what you did." She gazed into his eyes.

Lando exhaled before nodding, wrapping an arm around Ranaya's waist. He looked out the window beside them and scrunched his eyes, looking toward the castle and forest as if he saw people.

Ranaya stared out but saw nobody. Lando's eyesight had to be astounding for him to see so far away.

Lando's grip on her waist tightened, "People are awake. You need to get back to the castle before everybody wakes up."

Ranaya didn't want to go, but she knew she had to. The result of getting caught could end with Lando facing the gallows.

She began to un-wrap the cloak to place it on top of the trunk when Lando reached out to stop her.

"Keep it. It's cold out there—besides it will help you sneak into the castle easier since it's dark." Lando protested, wrapping it back around her shoulders.

"But won't you be cold?" Ranaya stared at him as he fastened the clasp at her neck.

"I have others," Lando gave her a bittersweet smile, his hands still lingering on her shoulders.

Ranaya's shoulder slumped as she stepped away from the elf. "When do you think we can see each other again?" she kept her gaze on Lando. She didn't want to go; not at all. She didn't want to leave Lando. She didn't want to be anywhere without him beside her.

The love she had for him seemed to get stronger and stronger each day. It never dimmed. And the more she fell in love with Lando the stronger her hatred toward Karik's actions became.

Life seemed to play a cruel trick on Ranaya and Lando. Allowing them to fall in love and then break them apart by a forced marriage.

"Remember yesterday when I said I would give you swimming lessons? Well those are today." Lando answered.

Ranaya gasped in delight and hugged him tightly. "I'll meet you around noon?"

Lando laughed and nodded, kissing her.

Ranaya pulled away reluctantly and prepared to go down the loft ladder.

Lando reached out and pulled the cloak's hood over her head.

She smiled before disappearing into the morning.

# Chapter 6

"Ranaya, my dear, where were you last night?" an annoying voice sounded behind Ranaya as she made her way through the gardens.

Couldn't she go anywhere and be rid of this king for once?

"Why is it any concern of yours, Karik?" Ranaya didn't even turn to look at him from behind. Her eyes traveled toward the stables. The doors were open and she could see Lando and Harry feeding the horses. She longed to be helping them. Maybe she could go help them and Karik would leave her alone.

Ranaya cried out as Karik seized her arm roughly and whipped her around to face him.

"Don't ever call me Karik. It's Your Majesty or Master." His voice was colder than ice.

"You certainly are not a Master of me and have nothing Majestic about you." Ranaya spat, her emerald eyes flashing.

"You will not speak to your future husband and king in that way, you ungrateful girl," Karik growled, his hold tightening on her arm.

Ranaya clenched her jaw at the pain but kept her glare on him. "You're not worthy to be called king. What you do to elves is inhuman."

"What's all the interest of elves lately, hmm?" Karik narrowed his eyes at her.

Ranaya didn't answer and only hoped Lando wasn't watching Karik's treatment of her.

No one was around at this hour, which made it all the while easier for Karik to say or do whatever he wished—that was except for Lando and Harry. She wished they would turn to look toward her and Karik.

Ranaya noticed Karik was staring at her wrapped hand. She quickly tried to put it behind her back but Karik let go of her arm and grabbed it.

"What happened here?" Ranaya flinched as he un-wrapped it. He wasn't gentle in the least and it hurt horribly. When Lando had put the salve and bandage on it, it hadn't hurt at all.

Karik scoffed as the bandage came loose and her burn was hit by the midday air. His eyes grew huge as he looked at the green paste covering her burn.

Ranaya panicked and tried to draw her hand away.

"This is elven." Karik's voice was dark as he stared at it. "Who doctored your hand?"

Fear was filling her body until she was almost paralyzed. Not fear for herself, but for Lando.

Ranaya's mouth opened to say something, but she shut it. She didn't know how to reply.

"Oh Princess, are you afraid?" Karik mocked. It was clear he was furious.

Not caring how much it hurt, all she knew was she had to get away from him. She snatched her hand away with the bandage and made a run for it, straight to the stables.

"Get back here, Ranaya Yarkish. You haven't answered me!" Karik snarled and ran after her.

Surely if she ran into the stables, Karik wouldn't hurt her in front of Lando and Harry?

Ranaya ran so fast she took a nosedive into the hay at the back of the stable, trying to stop. Lando and Harry came running up to her.

Lando was the first to reach her and gently pulled her away from the hay.

"Let go of me!" Ranaya screamed, thinking it was Karik. She struggled against him.

"Shhh, it's only me, Ranaya." Lando held onto her.

Ranaya stared up at him and relaxed if just for a second.

"Where is she? That miserable thing you call a princess!" Karik yelled in fury. He was a few yards behind them.

She stiffened in Lando's grasp, her fingers gripped at his sleeve.

"I won't let him hurt you, I promise," Lando whispered into Ranaya's ear.

"No you mustn't let him find you out," she protested, willing herself to let go of him and stand up, to face Karik head on.

Harry was staring at her and Lando, in question; as if he hadn't realized the two's affection before.

"No, Ranaya. I've put up with Karik treating you this way for far too long." His voice held vengeance.

Ranaya stared into his eyes and knew he was determined and unafraid of what he faced. She would not be able to talk him out of it this time.

Lando grasped her, under the elbows, and pulled her to her feet. Ranaya raised her chin to stare up at Karik as he approached them.

"How dare you run from me!" Karik snarled when he was close enough to Ranaya.

She was half expecting to be grabbed harshly by the king, but she was yanked away by Lando, and pushed behind him in blinding speed.

She gasped as Lando withdrew his sword and pointed it at Karik.

Harry backed into the wall with wide eyes. "Lando, what are you doing, my boy?" he gulped.

Karik gave Lando a nasty sneer. "You dare challenge me, boy?"

Lando continued to point the sword and glared. "You will not lay a finger on the Princess of Lakishea."

Karik laughed, "And who are you to tell me what I may and not do?"

"Lando, please, let it go," Ranaya gripped his arm. If he went any farther, he'd either be found out as an elf or worse--could be recognized as Landrian. It was a wonder Karik hadn't already figured out who he was.

Lando closed his eyes for a few seconds before putting his sword back in its sheath.

Ranaya stepped in beside him and stared at Karik. "What do you want from me?"

"What I want…," Karik mused. "What I want is to know why you have elven medicine on your hand!" he yanked her toward him.

Ranaya didn't even flinch. "What's it to you?"

She wished she could see Lando's face. Hopefully he was keeping his face straight.

"It's a lot to me, you wench!" Karik gave Ranaya a slap across the face. "You are mingling with elves and letting them use their medicine on you while you're engaged to marry me! They are heathens; worthless, no good, barbarians. They trick humans. Lure them into traps. They are my enemy and you're being friendly with them!" Karik was getting so furious; his face was turning red as a tomato. It was a wonder he didn't bust a vein.

"They are no such things!" Ranaya struggled against his grasp. "How dare you say such things!"

"If I ever see you with an elf, I will kill it. I swear." Karik growled. He was getting dangerously close to her face.

"Your Majesty, please release her," Harry pleaded.

"Very well." Karik threw Ranaya on the ground, causing her to roll to Lando's feet. "But if either of you two groomsmen say a word to anyone what you have witnessed, I will make sure you two are out of jobs and without reference." Karik turned and stormed out.

Ranaya was too afraid to speak, thinking Karik was still lingering around and could hear.

Lando knelt beside her and lifted her into a sitting position.

"Are you all right, Your Highness?" Harry frantically asked, coming to stoop beside Lando in worriment.

Ranaya didn't object his formal addressing. She was too stunned from what had happened. Her cheek was still smarting.

"I shouldn't have put my sword away. I'm so sorry, Ranaya." Lando hugged her close to him, placing a kiss on her forehead.

Harry blinked at the affectionate display. A princess and a stable boy... it wasn't supposed to be. He would not tattle, he loved his princess and respected her choices.

"Don't blame yourself. You didn't know he would do that." Ranaya caressed his face.

"Well Lando, I think you did enough work for today. After all that's happened, I think you deserve a break." Harry announced, slapping the elf's shoulder.

"Thank you, Master LeFroy." Lando nodded, and he took Ranaya's hand to pull her to a stand.

Harry smiled before walking into the tack room.

Ranaya sighed, feeling relieved to be rid of Karik.

"Now, how about that swimming lesson?" Lando asked, with a mischievous grin.

"I've been waiting all day." Ranaya laughed.

"What are we waiting for?" Lando took off at a run, Ranaya trying to catch up from behind him.

Karik was forgotten if only for a moment.

"I don't know if I want to do this Lando," Ranaya gulped, taking a step back from the edge of the water. Looking at it from where she stood, the murky water didn't look inviting. It looked more like a dark hole.

Lando had already jumped in and was swimming on his back. He made it look so easy that it exasperated the princess. His hair was floating out, revealing his pointed ears for all the world to see.

There wasn't anyone around except Ranaya and Lando, but Ranaya was afraid that someone would walk by and see the elf. It wasn't helping she was already nervous about being taught to swim.

"What are you afraid of, Ranaya?" Lando asked, with one those mischievous smiles of his.

"I'm--" Ranaya gasped as he disappeared under water. She got down on her knees and hands to peer into the water to find him. She spotted him as the light shining into the murky water.

Ranaya watched as the light moved around, and then frowned as he stopped glowing.

"Lando?" Ranaya asked, leaning over the rock until her hands and face were over the edge.

The water was still and she wondered what was taking him so long to surface.

Water splashed in front of her as Lando popped out of the water, splashing her face. She jumped back quickly in surprise.

"You were saying?" He grinned, his elbows propping on the rock in front of her. They were nearly nose to nose.

Ranaya's eyes narrowed, "I'm not scared." A playful smirk plastered on her face. She dipped her hand in the water and flicked water in the elf's face.

"Oh, really?" Lando didn't even blink, even as the water dribbled down his face. His grin grew larger as his eyes twinkled.

"Yes, really?" Ranaya teased. She was unconsciously leaning closer to the edge.

"Well then, Your Highness, I hope you don't mind me doing this." Lando grabbed Ranaya's arm so fast she didn't have time to react. She was in the water in mere seconds.

She shrieked in surprise and struggled to keep afloat. She felt the panic trying to settle in and she quickly tried to disperse it. If she panicked she knew she would drown herself. "Lando?!"

*Please, don't be too far away.*

Arms wrapped around her waist, and her face and shoulders were held above the surface. The panic in the pit of her stomach disappeared.

"See it's not that bad?" Lando whispered into her ear.

Ranaya didn't answer; she was too busy clinging to him. The feeling of her feet not touching the bottom made her wary.

"Now, let's teach you to float." Lando's grip lessened.

Ranaya gasped and held on tighter to his neck. "N-no, don't let go!" she squeezed her eyes shut.

"Relax; it will be fine. You'll see." Lando coaxed, though it wasn't helping.

"I can't relax when I'm dangling who knows how many feet above the stream floor!" Ranaya shook her head violently. "All I think of is falling down...down into the dark depths."

Lando sighed, "It's not that deep." He held onto her a little tighter. "No need to be dramatic."

"Then, pray tell, why did I almost drown last time you pulled me in?" Ranaya exclaimed. It was meant more as a joke but she knew as soon as she said it she shouldn't have.

Lando's face darkened at the mention of her almost fatal experience and he looked away from her. It had been he who pulled her in, but he hadn't known she couldn't swim.

Ranaya saw regret in his eyes. "Oh no, I didn't mean it like that." She let go of his neck with one of her arms, knowing now he was securely holding her and she would not fall. She placed her hand against his cheek.

Lando's eyes swiveled toward the rock ledge and stared at it, as if it were the most interesting thing in Lakishea.

"Lando, please look at me," Ranaya pleaded.

He didn't.

Ranaya took his chin and finally Lando met her eyes. "It wasn't your fault. You didn't know that I wasn't able to swim." Ranaya stared into his eyes. "In fact, if it wasn't for you I would have drowned. You saved me."

He sighed, "I still can't help but feel responsible."

"I know." Ranaya wrapped her loose arm back around his neck. "Now weren't you trying to teach me how to float?"

"If you'll let me," Lando playfully loosened his grip on her and let her go further into the water.

She let out a cry and tried to grab onto him, but he didn't let her.

"Be still and relax, then you won't sink," Lando explained.

Ranaya stilled and her heart pounded wildly at the thought of sinking.

Lando placed a hand over her hammering heart. She knew he could hear it with his elvish hearing.

It continued to thump against his hand as he lowered her into the water gradually with his other arm. "Do you trust me?" Lando asked.

"Yes," Ranaya breathed as Lando removed his hand from her heart. Water filled her ears and then she realized she was lying completely on her back in the water. It wasn't too bad—as long as Lando was still holding onto her.

"Not so bad is it?" Lando smiled.

"Not as bad as I thought," Ranaya sighed. In fact it felt wonderful. She felt as if she were weightless.

Lando swam away and suddenly she realized he wasn't holding onto her anymore. She was floating!

Her eyes were wide as she smiled. But then she frowned as she thought of how deep the water was. She tensed up.

"Ranaya, relax or you will sink!" Lando called out.

And Ranaya was doing exactly that. She flailed her arms in fear. Water filled her mouth.

Lando quickly swam toward her.

"Lan--," Ranaya gasped as she went under. The water filled her ears and made things sound odd. She didn't have long to think upon this though.

Lando grabbed onto her and pulled her up against him. "That was close."

"It was my fault," she leaned her head into his chest, trying to catch her breath. She could hear his heart. It was beating hard, probably out of excitement of her almost drowning again. It faltered a beat and Ranaya wondered why. Maybe, it was some Elvish trait. Were their heartbeats different than humans?

"All the same," Lando kissed her hair.

"I still wish to be taught to swim, not to just float." Ranaya halfheartedly teased. She forced a smile upon her face. Somehow, the abnormal beating of his heart made her worried. She tried to shake it off but had a very bad feeling, that maybe Lando was hiding something from her that had to do with his health.

"If you wish," Lando chuckled.

The next hour was spent teaching Ranaya to swim. And by the end of that hour she could at least keep herself from sinking. She was able to swim decently now.

"You did well," Lando encouraged as the two sat on the rock, drying off.

"I had a great teacher did I not?" Ranaya leaned her head on his shoulder.

"I wouldn't say I'm the best." Lando said, laying back to close his eyes.

Ranaya watched Lando and noticed that he looked exhausted. There was another red flag. He was usually so energetic. He could outrun her any day. She was always tired first, but not today. Swimming couldn't be that hard on you could it?

"Lando, are you feeling well?" Ranaya touched his arm. She had to find out if he was all right. Something was very off. She should have seen this earlier.

When he opened his eyes, they were filled with anguish. It scared Ranaya to see him so. It was gone as soon as it came. "Just catching an Elven cold most likely. It's nothing to worry about."

Ranaya decided not to bother him anymore about it, but it still stayed in the back of her mind.

There was a thunder of hoof beats coming up the path.

Ranaya jumped up as did Lando.

"Quick, get back into the water and to the reeds!" Lando exclaimed, referring to the reeds and greenery to the back of the stream where there was a bunch of rocks piled together. The whole stream was like a little cove.

They both jumped into the water and swam quickly to hide. Ranaya managed without drowning herself. They backed into the reeds, until they were covered from nose down.

Ranaya peeked through the reeds as the horse approached. To her dismay, the horse slowed to a trot. She shrunk closer to Lando, glancing at him. If Lando showed himself, he would be found out at once. The cloaked rider stopped right at the stream and dismounted to get a drink.

Ranaya narrowed her eyes to see who the rider was. Her eyes widened as the rider showed his face, rising up after cupping his hand into the water.

It was Dari, her older brother!

She wanted to spring out of the water to hug him, but fear of him finding Lando, and telling someone that Lando was an elf kept her in her place.

"Do you know who he is?" Lando whispered into her ear.

"It's my brother, who I haven't seen in two years. He had to go on a few missions around the borders of Lakishea," Ranaya breathed. She knew Lando heard her.

"You can swim up to him. I will stay here, until he's gone," Lando assured. It was like he knew what she was thinking.

"Are you sure?" Ranaya stalled. She didn't want to leave him.

Lando gave her a light push.

She gave in as the elf gave her a look, and swum up to the bank. "Dari!" she cried out.

The prince looked up in bewilderment but smiled as he realized who called his name. "Ranaya, what are you doing here?"

"Just taking a swim," she laughed. She wanted to hug him but didn't want to get him wet. She grabbed and held his hand instead.

"When did you learn to swim? Last time I was here, you swam like a rock." Dari raised an eyebrow.

Dari looked much like his little sister. His hair though, was a chocolate brown instead of auburn. His eyes were the same emerald color as Ranaya's.

"Well, I learned today." She glanced toward the reeds and then back to Dari.

"Oh, really, who taught you?" Dari teasingly asked. He picked her out of the water and sat her beside him.

"A friend," Ranaya blushed scarlet. She looked to the ground. If only Dari would stop asking so many questions. She would crack if he didn't.

Dari stared at her curiously. "Does this swimming and friend have to do with the person behind those reeds?"

Ranaya gasped in surprise. "How did you....?"

Lando was going to be found out. It made her sick to think about it. Maybe Dari wouldn't tell. He never told on her when they were children. But alas, they were grown now and this was a different matter than stealing cookies out of the kitchen or sneaking around without her slippers or corset.

"It was obvious, the way you kept glancing over there. I also saw some blonde hair peeking through." Dari laughed. "Please, tell your friend she or he can show their self."

Ranaya gulped. "I don't know if it's a good idea."

"Why, ever not?" Dari was mystified.

"Because he—he's a-," Ranaya stammered. What was she going to do?

"It's a he, is it now?" Dari was teasing her.

"Promise, you won't tell on him. Not a soul?" Ranaya begged.

"I don't know what I'm supposed to promise." Dari crossed his arms and gave her a look.

Ranaya sighed, "Lando, you can come out now."

There was silence and then Lando swam toward them. He kept himself almost fully immersed in the water. Dari stared, and looked as if he forgot how to blink.

"Lando, it's okay," Ranaya explained.

Lando hesitated before he fully rose up, to sit on the bank.

Dari's mouth dropped open, in surprise. "You're an elf?"

"Please, tell no one. He could be put to death if they found out who is he is." Ranaya took hold of the elf's hand to reassure him that Dari would not do anything.

"Why would he be put to death for being an elf?" Dari asked, looking confused.

"Haven't you heard?" Ranaya questioned her brother, her voice cracked in emotion. How could he not know about her engagement to the King of Zachavi and his brainwashing their father, Darius? Karik had somehow got permission to have full surveillance over Lakishea to find each and every elf hiding in the kingdom. Karik had made it his mission to humiliate and punish all of them, by cutting off their most highly prized possession of their persons. All elves wore their hair long. It was their pride and glory; cutting the hair was a sign of shame and humility.

"I've been gone for two years. I have heard no news of any sort lately. What's going on?" Dari took a hold of Ranaya's shoulders, his face serious.

Lando looked away, he was still wary of this prince. He could never be too careful.

"King Karik of Zachavi is visiting here." Ranaya began. Calling him king made Ranaya want to retch.

"What is he doing here?" Dari looked disgusted.

"I'm being forced to marry him. He's taking me away to Zachavi in less than two days." She looked into the water, her vision was blurring. She refused to cry! She wouldn't let herself. All it took was one look at Lando and it would be her undoing. She kept her gaze from the elf.

Lando breathed in sharply as if he was in pain and pressed his fist against his heart. He then quickly composed himself as if nothing had happened.

Ranaya turned to look at him, but Lando refused to look back. Tears pricked the back of her eyes and she had to blink several times to stop them. Why wouldn't he just tell her what was wrong?

"How could Father allow this? He knows what that king does to the elves of the Tarachi. How could he make you marry such a man?" Dari looked horrified. "I have to talk to him."

"It won't do any good. Karik has brainwashed him until Father actually allowed Karik to search through the entire kingdom for elves." Ranaya explained.

Dari stared again, at Lando, "How did you escape from being caught?" he asked the elf.

"Your sister helped me cover my ears with a little invention she said you made before you left." Lando smiled. Ranaya knew that the elf would warm up to Dari soon enough. He was looking more relaxed.

"Is that so?" Dari gave Ranaya a questioning look.

She smiled, despite trying not to cry. "Remember, those elf ears you made out of Harisc? I sawed off the tip to make them round."

"That's my clever girl," Dari cried and wrapped his arm around Ranaya.

She smiled and scooted over to sit next to Lando.

Lando smiled as Ranaya took his hand in her own. He was becoming relaxed now. He had nothing to fear from her brother.

Ranaya leaned her head on his bare shoulder; the heat of the sun was making her tired.

Dari's green eyes were full of surprise as he took in the scene before him. His little sister really loved this elf.

"I won't tell anyone of you being an elf. You have my word, that I will not to tell a soul. I will help anyway I can. I promise," and Dari truly meant it.

Ranaya looked up at her brother. "You do not understand how much that means to me." Lando's arm wrapped around Ranaya as the elf smiled.

Dari stood up and helped the two up. "Now, I believe Father and Mother will want to see me." He walked up to his horse that was patiently drinking from the stream.

"I will be seeing you, Ranaya." He mounted up. "I cannot believe how much you have grown. You're a full grown woman now. I have missed so much. It makes me wish I never had to leave the castle walls."

"I have changed little," Ranaya hugged him.

# Chapter 7

"Princess Ranaya! Your Highness, where are you?" Gertrude called out. The maid was half distraught and annoyed at the same time.

Ranaya was hiding and for a good purpose.

Because of Prince Dari's return and the celebration of her engagement to Karik, who was proposing to her tonight in front of the entire kingdom.

Yes for a very good reason indeed. Gertrude was trying to take the princess to her ball-gown fitting.

Ranaya was trying to delay it as long as possible. She wanted so badly to bolt out of the castle and get to the stables, fast as humanly possible.

She was worried about Lando. He had looked rather paler than usual. He was getting dark circles under his eyes. His whole demeanor was different. He looked so exhausted. It scared her to see him look so sick. It was like he went downhill after the swimming lessons. It had been only a day since Dari arrived. Lando had looked tired but nothing like this.

"Ranaya! Where is that child?" Gertrude exclaimed in impatience. She stopped right in front of Ranaya's hiding spot.

Ranaya stiffened behind the grand pillar. She would not get caught now. She hardly dared even to breathe until Gertrude was gone.

Ranaya sighed in relief as the maid continued down the hall, calling her name loud as ever.

She inched her way through the halls to sneak out of the castle. She wasn't sure if it was possible but she would try anyway.

Those guards weren't always the best watchers.

It only took her less than two minutes to escape them, and then she ran to the stables as fast as her legs would carry her.

Harry was the first she saw. He looked up as soon as he saw Ranaya coming. His expression was worried.

Ranaya's stomach twisted in knots. For him to look so solemn there had to be something wrong.

"What's the matter?" Ranaya asked. She was fearing the worst.

"The lad isn't faring well. I tried to get him to take a rest, but he refuses." Harry shook his head as he forked hay. "He listens to you."

Ranaya nodded and went on a hunt for the stubborn elf.

A tired groan confirmed where he was.

"Lando?" She followed the sound to the right back of the barn finding him grooming one of the stallions.

He looked down at her and then back to the horse. As if he didn't want her to see how he was really feeling.

Ranaya was shocked. For the few seconds she had been looking at him in the eyes she saw how much worse he was then yesterday. Lando was keeping something deadly serious from her. It was worse than she ever thought.

"Lando, you should rest. You're so tired." She touched his arm.

"And shouldn't you be getting ready for the ball tonight?" his tone was flat and emotionless.

"I wanted to make sure you were all right. Besides, I couldn't care less about the ball." She patted the roan stallion.

"It's held in your honor," Lando stated in a flat tone, not bothering to glance toward her.

"My honor is forced. I want you to be there with me." Ranaya looked down to the floor with a sigh.

"It's not possible for me to be there. I'm just a lowly stable hand; a commoner." His voice held sadness.

"I could make you a disguise! I could make you a Lord or Prince. And no you are not a lowly, commoner, stable hand. You're Landrian, a great warrior among your people." Ranaya forced him to look at her.

"A disguise wouldn't disguise who I am. Karik would straight away notice what I am. He might even realize I'm Landrian. It's a thousand wonders he doesn't recognize me even now." Lando paused in his grooming.

"Why does he want you dead so badly?" Ranaya asked. Her blood went cold at the thought of Lando dead. She didn't think she could bear it.

Lando's face was hard, "I killed both his grandfather and father who were plotting to destroy the Tarachi and its people. They're all evil rulers. Karik wants revenge; he was naught but a little boy when his father was killed. I fear he's worse than both of them together."

Ranaya blinked. Karik had to be 10 years older than Lando. "And how old was Karik's father when his grandfather was killed?"

Lando set his jaw. She could tell that he knew what she was getting at. "10."

"How old did you say you were again?" Ranaya took an intake of breath.

Lando smirked, "24." He gave her an innocent look and at that moment he didn't look sick anymore.

"How old are you truly?" Ranaya bit her lip. She wasn't sure if she wanted to know.

Lando's lips twitched and his eyes twinkled. He leaned down until his lips were an inch from her ear. His breath tickled her ear, and she shivered, fighting off the feeling. "I am exactly 240 years old."

Ranaya gasped in surprise. She was so surprised that she wobbled and almost fell backward if Lando hadn't grabbed her first.

"You—you." Ranaya stuttered, her eyes wide.

Lando looked amused. "So old?" he chuckled. "You're not but a babe compared to my age."

Ranaya swatted his arm. "I was only surprised."

"Elves are full of surprises," Lando whispered teasingly.

Ranaya huffed.

Lando frowned and placed a hand over his chest as if he were in pain. "You should be getting to your fitting."

"Only if you take a rest." Ranaya protested, taking the brush out of his hand.

Lando nodded. "Promise, you will meet me outside tonight?" he forced a smile through his pain.

"And do what? Will you even be able to make it anywhere? You look positively horrid." Ranaya stood on her toes and kissed the bottom of his chin.

"I may not be able to dance with you in the castle but we can do as we please in the gardens. This is the last day and night I will ever see you and I will see you even if it kills me to do so." Lando confirmed. He kissed her and was reluctant to let her go. "I have something to give you tonight."

Ranaya didn't want to leave him. Just having Lando bring up the part of this being the last day with him made her feel horrible.

"You better go." Lando said.

"Get some rest," Ranaya choked before running out of the stables.

"Hold still, Your Highness." Gertrude scolded.

Ranaya could not stop fidgeting, no matter how much she tried. Pins were poking into her head as the lady's maid forced her hair up into the most stylish up do. It made Ranaya's head feel heavy having so much hair piled up. Did they expect her to walk about with a beehive on top of her head?

"It's impossible to be still when you have things jabbing you into the head." Ranaya closed her eyes in discomfort, trying to sound pleasant as    she gritted her teeth.

"If you were still Milady you would not be jabbed so," Gertrude fretted and patted her hair down, and then placing the crown on top of her head.

Ranaya could scarcely breathe from being caged into the whale bone corset when she stood up. The dress she wore was too formal for her tastes. It was red satin with flowing sleeves that went down to the floor. There were beads all over the dress. She hardly recognized her reflection in the mirror. She looked—like a princess. Probably for the first time in her life that is.

"That Zachavian King will be blown away," Gertrude nodded, putting a pair of silver slippers on the floor for Ranaya to slip into.

Ranaya's stomach churned. She didn't want to please Karik. She was wondering more about Lando's reaction.

A horn blew, signaling that the ball was beginning. It was supposed to be the announcement of the royal family's entrance.

"Blessed bits, you're late!" Gertrude gasped, shooing Ranaya out of the door. All the while, Ranaya walked through the halls, she was dreading the moment she had to walk through the ballroom holding Karik's hand, pretending she cared for him.

All of the royals were in the ballroom when Ranaya arrived. Only Karik stood, waiting impatiently for her.

"You're late," he growled, grabbing her arm in a rough manner.

Ranaya forced a smile and made herself look straight ahead as they were announced. She scanned the crowd with her eyes. She half hoped to see Lando in the crowd. It was silly of her to wish such a thing. The guards wouldn't let him pass. He was commoner to them and only royals were allowed in.

"Our Princess Ranaya Yarkish escorted by King Karik Forde of Zachavi."

Ranaya kept her forced smile plastered as she passed her family. Dari gave her a sympathetic smile.

Women were gossiping about her as they passed. She was sure they had heard of her relationship with a stable boy, while she was supposed to be courting a king.

Truthfully, Ranaya didn't care what anyone thought anymore—that is about herself. Lando on the other hand, wasn't to be talked about like scum on a bucket.

"I've heard he's a looker all right. No wonder the princess has her claws into him. What must the Zachavian King think of her sneaking about?"

She could hear every nasty remark about herself and Lando. Karik chuckled beside her.

"It seems everyone knows your little secret." He didn't sound surprised at all, maybe even pleased. As if he wanted to humiliate her in front of everyone. No doubt he had spread the rumor.

Ranaya didn't reply.

The night dawdled slowly and Ranaya was bored out of her mind. Countless princes and lords came to ask her to dance but she refused them all, deciding she preferred to be a wallflower. She didn't care if the ball was held in her honor. She danced with Dari, but it hardly counted. She felt that if she danced with anyone, she would be betraying Lando.

Ranaya was very aware of Karik's glares that were sent her way. She waited one hour before bolting outside. She couldn't wait to get away from it all.

The guards gave her a suspicious glance but it didn't stop her from going out of the castle. If they found out where she was actually going and whom she was to meet she would be in over her head.

Ranaya disappeared into the night quickly and sprinted into the gardens, hoping Lando would wait for her.

"Lando," she whispered into the night. She knew he would hear her calling even if she kept her voice quiet. His hearing was absolutely amazing.

"Yes?" a familiar voice whispered back, behind Ranaya in her ear.

Ranaya opened her mouth, a scream building up inside her.

Lando quickly covered her mouth with a hand to smother it. "Ssshh."

She pushed his hand away gently and twirled around to stare at him. His eyes held a mischievous glint in the moonlight.

He was wearing a cloak with a hood covering his head to keep himself from glowing. He also wore gloves. His face was the only thing that glowed. There wasn't any way to keep it from doing so.

"You scared me," Ranaya accused but smiled nonetheless. She was so happy to see him she forgave him instantly. She half expected him not to make it. He had looked so exhausted when she had last seen him.

Now, looking into his eyes, he looked tired but not exhausted.

"It's an elf thing." He grinned. He took her hand in his.

Ranaya knew that this night would turn out a whole lot better then she thought.

Ranaya reveled in the feel of her hand in Lando's though she wished he wasn't wearing gloves. She missed feeling the smooth skin of his bare hands.

Tonight was probably the last night she would ever see or be with Lando. Karik was taking her away to Zachavi.

Ranaya wouldn't even get to see her family but on special occasions and holidays. She knew she would miss Lakishea and her family, but she would miss Lando twice as much as everyone else combined.

She had vowed as a child that she would never fall in love. She never made friends with the stuffy and coy princes. The only friend she had ever had was her brother, Dari. But then he went away, and she had no one for years. That is until she met the elf walking beside her.

Lando had become Ranaya's dearest friend and much more. She could be herself with him. She didn't have to watch what she said or did. He accepted her the way she was. He didn't expect less or more of her. She couldn't have a better friend than him. Around Lando she could let her guard down and not be ashamed of her weakness. When she was around him she felt safe and secure from Karik. As much as it aggravated her to feel like that, she realized sometimes she needed to let her feelings show. She wanted to fight the feeling of being protected by Lando when Karik was nearby when she was supposed to be protecting him.

Sure as sun shines, Lando was her dearest friend that she had fallen hard in love with. A warm feeling flooded inside her at the thought. She was just as sure he felt the same.

Ranaya's hand tightened around Lando's. She would keep the memory of this night in her heart to remember the rest of her life. She knew that even when she grew old and gray, thoughts of Lando would come to haunt her.

Lando looked down at her and smiled. For a few seconds the tired Lando before her disappeared and the old Lando with endless energy was back.

"I will miss you so much," Ranaya tried to keep her voice even. She felt tears prick the back of her eyes as she met his eyes.

As quick as that the tiredness crept back into Lando, his eyes were filled with sorrow so deep it was like a knife twisting itself into her chest.

A gasp escaped her lips and her empty hand went up to clutch her chest. A shooting pain ripped into her heart.

Lando's sorrowful look was suddenly replaced with concern and he grabbed onto Ranaya. "Are you all right?"

Leave it to Lando to worry about her when he was supposed to be worrying about his own health. He was the one that was sick.

Ranaya was able to tear her eyes from his. "I think so." She forced a smile, trying not to look directly into his eyes. "I had a sudden pain in my chest. It's gone now."

Lando stopped them then, his eyes widened. "It was me—I'm so sorry. I didn't..." he trailed off

"You didn't what?" Ranaya tried to probe.

He acted like he hadn't heard and his sorrowful look was replaced with his familiar mischievous twinkle. He didn't want to talk about it for some odd reason

"Will you give me the honor of this dance?" He held her hand up and bowed over it with such elegance she could have sworn that moment he was of noble blood.

Ranaya's eyes became wide in surprise. She wasn't expecting this. Not being able to find her voice, she nodded and smiled.

He placed his unoccupied hand on her waist and frowned. Most likely, noticing how gauntly thin she had become.

Ranaya could hide it with her clothes, but she knew she was boney and needed to gain weight. It was impossible to eat when she had to stare at Karik from across the stable. She lost her appetite every time.

"You need to try to eat," Lando said, his expression genuinely worried. He knew she wasn't eating right.

Ranaya lowered her gaze for a few seconds after she placed her injured hand on his shoulder. It was no longer bandaged. It wasn't healed up yet, but she hadn't wanted to take any chances on anyone questioning it being wrapped up. She sighed.

Lando then twirled her around in a dance. It was fast but not too fast.

Ranaya couldn't remember when she had had so much fun dancing. It was supposed to be boring. With Lando it was thrilling. Like floating and sailing in the clouds

She laughed when she had to duck under his arm.

The music flowed out into the garden. The first few melodies were fun and fast paced. ever so often it would start to thunder.

The music was slowing down, making it impossible to dance fat.

Lando smiled and pulled her into a slow dance.

These were the ones that were the most boring to Ranaya...usually. Tonight, she found that dancing slow was amazing.

She couldn't draw her eyes away from Lando's glassy blue gaze.

He held her close as if she would disappear from him. He looked like he was trying to keep tears from trickling down his face. "Love is an understatement of what I feel for you, Ranaya Yarkish."

Ranaya's hand tightened around his. "I will never forget you." She too felt tears coming at bay.

Lando gave a shuddering exhale.

Ranaya laid her head down against him, closing her eyes. Tears were threatening to overwhelm her.

# Chapter 8

Ranaya stayed as she was for a while. Lando's heartbeat was the only sound besides the quiet music coming from the castle.

His heartbeat wasn't as steady as she remembered it to be. It often skipped or tripped over itself as she listened. She tried her best not to think about it, but she knew there was something deadly wrong with Lando. Before she knew it she was crying.

Her tears trickled down her face and landed on Lando's dark blue tunic.

Ranaya had to stop, or she would soak him. "I'm sorry I'm acting like this," she said, opening her eyes up. She tilted her face up to stare at him.

They weren't dancing anymore. Lando let go of her waist to wipe a tear from her face. "What is there to be sorry for?" He questioned as he caressed her face. There were tears in his own eyes though they never fell.

Thunder boomed in the distance and a breeze blew across the garden, making the flowers dance. It was a signal of a storm brewing.

"For having to leave you."

Lando tightened his hold on Ranaya's hand. If he squeezed any tighter it would have hurt. "You have no way to stop this." His voice was thick.

At that moment, the sky decided to let loose and rain poured down.

Lando pulled her after the stables and they made a quick sprint for cover.

Ranaya was shivering by the time they got into the door. She covered it up quickly as Lando lit a lantern. She didn't want him to notice. He would no doubt try to give her his cloak, she couldn't have that.

They were alone, except for the horses. Harry was home with his wife and children tonight.

She sat down on a bale of hay, absently, while her eyes never left the elf.

"I have something I want to give to you," Lando gave her a light kiss on her brow.

Ranaya closed her eyes and relished in the feeling. Everything he said or did was precious to her. If only, she could bottle up every memory of him inside her, and never forget.

Lando went up the loft ladder and meddled in his trunk.

She was curious to know what he was doing. What could he possibly want to give her? He had given her so much already.

When he came back, he held a small wooden box that fit in his palm.

Ranaya stared in question at it before glancing into Lando's eyes.

He sat beside her and turned to face her. "This was my mother's. It was given to her by my father when I was born. She gave it to me right before the Zachavian raiders killed her." Lando's expression was bittersweet.

He opened the box slowly, to reveal a ring. It was the most beautiful thing Ranaya had ever seen.

It had a delicate emerald silhouette of a tree. The base behind the tree was opal like which shimmered different colors when angled different ways. It had a white gold band.

Ranaya gasped. He couldn't mean he was giving this to her.

Sure enough, he took it out of the box and slipped it onto her ring finger, on her left hand. Had he meant to do that?

"Lando, you cannot mean to give this to me." Ranaya protested, feeling dazzled and shocked, all at the same moment. "You should save it for the one you marry." The thought of him marrying someone else made her stomach churn, but she couldn't think so selfishly. She was leaving him tomorrow, and he was bound to find someone else in his long life span, most likely another elf like himself. He could live to be over a thousand years.

Lando stared at her as if she grew two heads, and then his brow wrinkled and his mouth set stubbornly. "There is no other. There won't ever be another for me, Ranaya. My mother gave this to me to give to my soul mate. It belongs to you. Will you marry me here and now?" He closed his hand over hers.

Ranaya was speechless. All she could do was hug him. "I love you, Landrian, but how can we marry with no minister? What about Karik?"

He smiled at the use of his real name. "You won't ever be truly his wife if you marry me now. And I know you Ranaya. You will find a way to escape before the time comes. He can't be bound to someone already bound to another. And if you can't escape before the time comes, I will find you, I promise." He took her hand then. "The Elves don't need ministers to marry them. We speak the vows among ourselves underneath the ancient twin trees in the Joined Trees Grove, with the Lord as our witness." He held her hand near the lantern and gestured to the ring.

"I want to say yes," she whispered. She looked at the ring and was puzzled at first until the most amazing sight surrounded her. The ring was reflecting hundreds of multicolor silhouettes of trees, and speckled in between the normal trees were giant trees twisted around each other, the twin trees. They surrounded the both of them.

"This ring reflects the symbol of my people when placed by a flame in darkness. The tree symbolizes life and hope in the darkest times. The trees are sacred to the elves and a reminder from God. It shows the sacred wood where the elven race was created, where before the Zachavians took over the grove all wedding ceremonies took place. We would stand before the Joined Trees and become a joined soul, just as the trees have. When we couldn't go back to that place we made rings like these so we could all be married there." He explained, taking both her hands in one of his.

"And now, in this sacred wood, we will be joined too." His speech became grander. "Like the Great Joined Trees in the Sacred Grove, let me be joined to this woman, the beautiful, loving Ranaya. Let her always be joined with me, no matter what distance, we will never be truly separated. Like the earth and the moon, let us be tied together by our Lord God and his son Jesus, who showed us how to truly love."

He then twined their hands together touching the ring. "Now, Ranaya. Repeat after me. Like the Great Joined Trees in the Sacred Grove, let me be joined to this man, Landrian."

With tears in her eyes she repeated and paraphrased "Like the Great Joined Trees in the Sacred Grove, let me be joined to this man, the amazing and wonderful Landrian."

At her addition he smiled, looking deep into her eyes before continuing "Let him always be joined with me, no matter what distance, we will never be truly separated."

She repeated it, and he gave her the last line to say. "Like the earth and the moon, let us be tied by our Lord God and his son Jesus, who showed how to truly love." She smiled at him.

"Now you would give me my ring, but as you don't ha—"She cut him off before he could finish.

"It's not a ring, but will this do?" She reached back and unclasped the necklace that held the key to the tree that stored all her treasures. She placed it in Lando's hand.

He hooked it around his neck. "It will, and I will take care of it. I promise."

"I know you will." Ranaya fought a shiver of cold as she stared down at the ring. Wind blew through the cracks in the stable doors and Ranaya gave in and shuddered against Lando. She had forgotten how cold she was in her excitement.

"Lando, I will be an old lady and you won't even have aged." Ranaya frowned. The lifespan difference was a big issue. What were they going to do?

"When an elf binds him or herself to a human, the elf's life span is instantly cut off to only be as long as a human's." Lando smiled as if it was the greatest thing in the world.

"Aren't you upset that you will not have lived your thousand of years?" Ranaya pressed herself to his side, trying to become warm from his body heat without him noticing what she was doing.

"I'd rather live a short life span with you rather than live centuries without you." Lando took her hand in his and jerked backward in surprise. "You're positively freezing." He chastised, feeling how cold she was.

"No I--" Ranaya tried to protest. He ignored her, completely.

He ushered her to the loft, where the wind couldn't hit them. He wrapped a blanket around her as they sat down. She sighed thankfully and leaned her head back into his shoulder.

She was getting really tired, but was trying to fight it off. She wanted as much time with Lando as possible, especially on their wedding night, and the last night she might ever see him.

"I know you're sleepy." Lando said. It was like he read her mind or something.

"How did you know?" Ranaya sighed. She didn't want to have to go back into the castle.

"It's easy to read your body language." His arms wrapped around her, allowing her to put her full weight against him.

"I don't want to go back into the castle. I don't want to leave Lakishea. I want to stay here, married to you." Ranaya protested.

"Ranaya, you will always be married to me. But I didn't say you had to leave," Lando   grew solemn.

Ranaya worried about what would happen if they were caught alone together, but her eyes were getting so heavy she knew she wouldn't make it back to her room. "I should go."

"You are my wife, you can stay here." Lando didn't seem to want to let her go either.

Ranaya didn't argue and yawned. She truthfully didn't care what they thought of her. They could accuse her and call her a trollop, but it wouldn't bother her. She knew she wasn't doing anything indecent, especially because now they were married. Anything that should happen on their wedding night would be fine. What she worried about was what would become of Lando if he was charged for dishonoring the princess. He would surely be put to death.

Lando laid his head against hers.

"Will you sing for me, one last time?" Ranaya pleaded. She wanted to hear him once more before she could never hear him again. She could hardly imagine never hearing his voice or seeing his face again. It was too horrible to bear. She had to find a way back to him.

Lando smiled and pulled her down to the hay, until they were laying down side by side, facing each other. She stared at him in wonderment.

He began to sing. It was even more beautiful than the other two times. He voiced both happy and sad words in his language. When Ranaya knew she was about to fall asleep, she kissed him into silence so she wouldn't fall asleep.

Ranaya awoke slowly. She felt so peaceful even though she was on a bed of hay. Her head rested on something solid and warm—Lando's chest.

She looked up at him and was surprised to see him still asleep.

Ranaya rose up but then realized she was trapped between Lando's arm… Not that she was complaining. She smiled and settled on letting Lando sleep until he woke up.

Her smile instantly faded as it hit her, like bricks. She was leaving in a few hours; leaving her family and Lando, her husband. It seemed so strange to call him that, but so right.

She took in a shaky breath as she stared at Lando. She studied his features for almost an hour. Was it possible to permanently brand someone's face into your brain? So you could always remember exactly what they looked like.

She studied every contour, even the way his hair strung out everywhere when he slept; tickling her cheek a little. His ears were fully exposed to her.

Ranaya didn't feel she was over exaggerating, when she thought he was the most beautiful creature she'd ever laid eyes on.

It was at that moment, Lando's eyes opened slowly and he looked straight into Ranaya's green eyes. He didn't look surprised to have caught her     staring.

He looked as if he hadn't slept in months, instead having just wakened. He had dark circles under his eyes; but Ranaya didn't have long to think about it as Lando smiled at her. "Good morning, my beautiful wife."

As much as she hated it, tears streamed down her face. She buried her face into his chest with a sobbing heave.

Lando held onto her tightly. He didn't say a word, knowing there wasn't much he could say.

The stable doors opened then and Ranaya stilled against him, in fear of them being caught.

Lando's grip tightened around her as boots sounded next to the loft ladder.

Ranaya held her breath. If this was Karik then they would be in some deep trouble.

Ranaya clutched Lando's arm tightly as the owner of the boots climbed up the loft. Horrible visions of what they would do to Lando if they were found flashed in her head.

"Ranaya? Lando?" Dari poked his head up into the loft in surprise, to see the two clinging to each other, as if their lives depended on it.

Ranaya and Lando both exhaled in relief.

"Ranaya, you need to get back to the castle, before someone knows you're missing. I had to tell them you went

to bed last night so no one would wonder where you were."
Dari gave them a sympathetic smile.

Ranaya nodded and reluctantly unlocked herself from the
elf. "I'll see you later." She barely whispered in defeat.

# Chapter 9

"Ranaya dear, stop dawdling. You're on your way to your betrothed's kingdom. You act as if it's a death sentence instead." Queen Helen, her mother chided, trying to hurry her daughter along the cobble stones, toward the awaiting carriage.

"At least let me say goodbye, to my friends," Ranaya said in a monotone voice.

And husband....

Her eyes instantly were drawn to the elf standing in the crowd, with a forlorn expression.

"Very well," Helen sighed and stepped aside to stand beside King Darius.

Ranaya couldn't help but notice Dari shooting daggers at Karik's back.

She hugged Harry and even Gertrude who was crying, and said she would miss her. The older woman had requested to stay in Lakishea, where her family lived. Karik had promised another lady's maid for Ranaya. The princess didn't really care if she had a maid, but she kept her tongue silent. It was best not to infuriate Karik further.

Ranaya pushed through the crowds, until she was face to face with Lando.

"I guess this is it then." Lando looked down at her with pain in his eyes. The pain cut Ranaya to the core again and made her feel that same sharpness in her chest. She couldn't look away even in pain.

"Yes," Ranaya whispered.

He wrapped his arms around her and embraced her. "I will find you. I promise it. Karik can't keep you there for long," he said softly in her ear. He said it so quietly that no one heard but her.

Ranaya's arms tightened around him at his words. "I will watch for you." She tried to keep her voice even.

Lando gave her a sad smile before kissing her so quickly not a soul, but the people standing beside them saw it.

"It's time to go, Princess." Karik was waiting in the carriage impatiently. Ranaya was thankful he hadn't seen the affectionate display between her and Lando.

Lando fingered the ring he had given Ranaya from around her neck. She had put it on a chain, so not to draw attention to it on her hand.

With a small cry, she let go of Lando and backed away.

Lando grabbed her hand as if to try to keep her with him, but her hand slipped out of his when she became out of reach.

Ranaya could see tears forming in the elf's eyes and she felt some of her own threaten to come down.

With one last hug to Helen and Dari and a glare for Darius, she got into the carriage. She was careful not to glance at Karik.

Lando had stepped forward to the front of the crowd when Ranaya turned to look behind her as the carriage rolled.

Something was wrong with Lando. He clutched his chest with his eyes squeezed shut, and his teeth clenched so hard his veins showed in his neck.

"No," Ranaya whispered. She already was fumbling with opening the carriage door.

And then Lando collapsed onto the ground.

"No!" she screamed and scrambled out of the carriage. She landed on her hands in knees onto the cobblestones, but was too blinded by fear for Lando that she didn't feel the pain from falling out of a moving carriage.

The crowds stepped away from the fallen man and were gaping as the princess threw herself down beside him; taking the stableboy in her arms protectively.

"Lando!" Ranaya cradled his head in her lap. "Please look at me." She sobbed. She pushed the hair that had fallen into his eyes away.

Lando opened his eyes slowly. They were filled with agony. "I—I'm glad to have met you, my dearest Ranaya. Know that I will always love you." Each word was an effort for him.

"Sir Lando!" It was Harry who dropped down beside them. Other than being head over the stables, Harry was a Physician to all the palace workers.

Ranaya was grabbed sharply and pulled away from Lando. "No! Lando! I can't leave him! He needs me!" she screamed wildly, and beat at Karik's chest.

It didn't faze the king as he pulled her back into the carriage rather roughly.

This was the beginning of Ranaya's nightmare.

# Part 2

# The Legacy of Elwood

# Chapter 10

"Welcome to your new home, Princess." Karik spread his arms wide, showing the large castle in front of Ranaya. As always, his voice was sugary sweet. The way he had welcomed her sounded sarcastic. He wasn't hiding his dislike to his beloved betrothed.

Ranaya wasn't impressed. To her, the overly large castle with its many towers, looked like a cold prison; dark and dreary.

Everything it was supposed to look like. Ranaya didn't expect it to look cheery.

They had been traveling for days through Glander and Irlandia. They had past hills, mountain paths, and rivers. Ranaya's back was killing her. It wasn't helping she already didn't feel so well.

She didn't answer Karik as he helped her out of the carriage. She walked toward the entrance gates with a tired drag.

Two solemn guards stood on each side, their faces void of any expression. Ranaya was taken aback by their features and the realization. Their hair was hacked off and revealed their pointed ears. They were some of the enslaved Tarachi elves Karik kept around.

They quickly opened the gates for her to go through. Ranaya could feel them staring at her. She wasn't sure why. Was it because she was new to Zachavi, or because they knew she was being forced to do something she didn't want, just like they were?

She could hear Karik's quick steps behind her. She walked faster. She didn't want to be near him right now… or ever really, for that matter.

"Hello, Mistress," an elf curtsied rather quick and sharp. It was as if she were afraid to be struck if she wasn't trying her hardest to be mannerly.

It made Ranaya all the more nervous in the Zachavian Castle. Elves were everywhere. All the servants were elven with hacked or shaved heads. It made the girl sick to watch how they served Karik. They were quick to please and skittish as if they expected a beating if they did something the least bit wrong.

Ranaya had the distinct feeling that if she didn't do what Karik wanted, she too would be punished. Not that she cared what he did. She would not be pushed into doing or being something she wasn't.

Much to her annoyance Karik stood right behind her. "This is Sharissa, your new maid."

Ranaya smiled at the elf, wishing the young maid would loosen up. It was probably hard with Karik around. Was the elf always this stiff?

Sharissa glanced at Karik before letting her eyes settle onto her new Mistress.

Karik didn't seem to have much patience as he clapped his hands.

Two elves came walking in with Ranaya's trunk of belongings.

"Sharissa, please take Princess Ranaya to her quarters. I'm sure she's exhausted from her trip." Karik made a motion with his hand before walking off to shout at a few elves who were scrubbing the floors.

Ranaya's skin crawled at his harsh words of future punishment if they didn't make it sparkle.

"Come along, Mistress," Sharissa said, turning to walk through the halls.

Ranaya followed behind the elves with her trunk. "Please Sharissa, call me Ranaya."

Sharissa looked absolutely horrified as did the other two elves. "I must call you Mistress or Your Highness. If I shan't, I will be punished within an inch of my life." She exclaimed in terror. "You must know what kind of man His Majesty is."

Ranaya said no more as Sharissa opened doors to a beautiful chamber. Ranaya without delay laid down on the canopy bed.

The rooms that were hers were stunning and yet she knew that this was to become her prison. No matter how beautiful it was to the eyes.

When Ranaya woke she felt dread. It was a horrible dread that seeped through her entire being. Everything seemed so surreal.

Marrying Lando secretly, and then the next day being ripped away to Zachavi to live with her supposed betrothal Karik. It was a lot to take in.

Ranaya clasped the ring on the chain that was around her neck. Visions of Lando collapsing to the cobblestones flashed through her mind.

A gasping sob threatened to escape her lips, but she held back. Not knowing if he was alive and well or dead killed her inside.

She rose up from the bed, taking the lit lantern that was on the nightstand to walk over to her trunk. She fumbled with the latch until it clicked and raised the lid to stare at her belongings she took with her.

Her eyes were drawn to find the neatly folded navy cloak hidden under her dresses. She pulled it out and clutched it to her chest. The only other thing besides the ring that made her feel a tad bit closer to Lando in this terrible castle and kingdom.

The cloak still smelled like him (that wonderful woodsy smell).

Ranaya unfolded it and wrapped it around herself as a shiver of cold ran through her. She rested her head in her arms on top of the trunk, not wanting to move.

The door swung open and Sharissa came in carrying a tray. The maid stopped short as she saw the princess lying over the trunk as if dead.

"Your Highness, are you all right?" Sharissa sounded panicked.

Ranaya startled, and she stood up at once. "Ye—yes, I'm all right."

Sharissa didn't look convinced as she sat the tray on a coffee table and gestured for Ranaya to sit down on the velvet settee across from them.

Ranaya grabbed the lantern and placed it on the table.

Sharissa stared at the cloak as if she had never seen one before. "I know it's not my place Milady, but may I ask where you gained this particular cloak?" she looked toward the door and sat down beside Ranaya.

Ranaya's eyes widened, in surprise. Did the maid know who it belonged to? "I—it was given to me by a stable hand." It was the truth. She couldn't help but smile. Indeed, a stable hand, but not just any stable hand. It was Landrian himself in the flesh.

"You seem fond of this stable hand." Sharissa smiled as she fixed Ranaya a cup.

Tears sprang up in Ranaya's eyes. "I would be with him now if it wasn't for Karik."

Sharissa frowned as she handed the cup to Ranaya.

"Thank you," Ranaya said and shakily took a sip. It wasn't sweet enough so Ranaya leaned over to pop another sugar cube into the tea cup.

Much to Ranaya's horror, the lantern light caught the ring around her neck just right and reflected.

Sharissa gasped. "Where did you get that?" she asked in a strangled voice.

Ranaya pressed her hand against the ring to make the images stop.

Ranaya leaned back into the settee with a deep sigh. "It came from the stable hand."

"A stable hand couldn't possess such a ring. It is elven crafted and fit for royalty itself or someone of high stature." Sharissa said in a gentle voice.

Ranaya closed her eyes. "It belonged to an elf. His name was Lando or known to your kind as Landrian."

"Landrian?" Sharissa gasped in shock, "The great warrior, General... himself?"

Ranaya was puzzled by how this maid was acting. It was as if Ranaya had just told her the moon doesn't shine on its own.

Ranaya slowly nodded with a soft sigh, "My husband." She breathed.

Sharissa looked like she was seconds from swooning. "Husband?" she blinked then blinked a second time. It was like she was trying to process all she heard. "But you're engaged to His Majesty."

Ranaya panicked. "You can't tell Karik. He must never know." The tea cup rattled violently in her hands .Sharissa wouldn't give her away would she?

Sharissa smiled, taking the cup from Ranaya's hand, taking the princess's in her own. "You are planning on trying to run away aren't you?" the maid's smile faded and turned into a frown.

"I want to." Ranaya wondered why this made the elf frown.

Sharissa took a sharp intake of breath. "You will never make it as far as two inches from the castle gates. If His Majesty finds you escaping, you would be severely punished.

The same as for me or any of the Tarachians enslaved to this castle."

"Punished?" Ranaya was unnerved by the maid's expression. It was so intense. Her eyes were filled with horror and tears shone in her eyes.

"You are taken to the dungeon and to endure a severe beating or to be flogged. You are scarred to remember your treachery." Sharissa placed the cup on the table, fixing her gaze back on Ranaya.

Ranaya covered her mouth to muffle a gasp. She knew Karik was evil but how far would he go?

"I must try to get away. I have to get to Lando." Ranaya protested.

Sharissa bowed her head, taking up the tray. Without a word she stepped out of the room and was gone, leaving Ranaya to her thoughts.

How was she going to escape?

An idea struck her. She would write a letter to Dari and ask him for advice.

# Chapter 11

R anaya scribbled…..

*Dear Dari,*

*I have just arrived to the Zachavian Castle…*

*It's everything I knew it would be; cold, dark, and dreary. You couldn't imagine how many elves are enslaved in this fortress. It sickens me to see them bending to every will. If they don't do as Karik orders they are punished within an inch of their life.*

*I'm hoping you will look out for Lando for me. Tell me how he is fairing? I was so scared when he collapsed.*

*I know my hopes are useless, but just maybe I can somehow escape marrying Karik. I can't marry him. I can never love a man so evil. My heart belongs to Lando and only Lando. I feel it and I know it's true. I'm going to find a way and I will come back to him.*

*Please don't tell our parents.*

*Ranaya*

Ranaya placed the quill down with a sigh. She folded and placed the letter into an envelope.

A throat cleared behind her and she jumped in her chair in front of the desk. Ranaya turned to see Sharissa looking around sheepishly.

"Whatever is the matter?" Ranaya sat the letter down onto the desk and got up.

Sharissa quickly jerked her attention to the princess. "His Majesty requests your presence in the dining hall. I've come to help you change your gown."

Ranaya pulled the navy cloak tighter to herself. "If His Majesty insists." The title left a bad taste in her mouth. She made her way to her trunk to pull out her next best dress other than her ball gown.

"Oh no, Your Highness. His Majesty wants you to wear a gown from your new wardrobe." Sharissa sauntered to an armoire that Ranaya hadn't even noticed until now.

Ranaya's nose crinkled in disgust as the maid opened the armoire to reveal the laciest and most beaded gowns the girl had ever seen. They were so fancy and nothing like had ever worn.

She mentally groaned to herself as she searched through the gowns to find one she liked. It took her a while but finally, she found an emerald green dress with flowing sleeves and pearls on the bodice. It was the least fancy of the bunch.

"Lovely choice," Sharissa smiled as she laid the dress onto the bed with the proper undergarments.

Ranaya nodded with a tiny smile and undid the navy cloak to fold it neatly and place it back in the trunk. Sharissa began getting the princess ready.

Ranaya tried to protest she could dress herself, but dropped it as Sharissa ignored her arguing.

"If I do not help you get ready I will get in trouble with the Master for not doing my job." The maid helped Ranaya into her dress after getting rid of the wrinkled traveling dress and having Ranaya put on more undergarments, to improve the princess's form, to which Ranaya was not thrilled about. She hated to wear such uncomfortable things.

By the time Sharissa got to Ranaya's hair Ranaya could scarcely breathe from the whale bone corset being so tight. She didn't think she'd ever worn one as tight before.

"Sharissa, can't my corset be loosened a little?" Ranaya winced as the elf pinned her hair up high on her head like a beehive.

"It cannot be done. His Majesty wishes you to look your part as the future Queen. The tight corset will help your posture." Sharissa finished her hair and placed a pair of slippers in front of Ranaya.

"It may help my posture, but I cannot act like a future Queen if I have passed out from not being able to breathe." Ranaya sighed as she slipped her feet into the heeled slippers.

Sharissa gave her an understanding look. "I know, it must be torturous, I wish I wasn't forced to do things I wish not to do. I am not capable of having my own mind in this castle or any part of Zachavi. I am a mere slave here. If I do or say anything out of my line it ends badly." Sharissa looked down.

Ranaya felt horrible for complaining when Sharissa had it much worse than she did. It was in that moment Ranaya decided; when she escaped she would take Sharissa with her. The maid deserved freedom as well as all the rest did.

Ranaya wished somehow she could free all the elves in Zachavi.

"Come along. His Majesty is waiting." Sharissa broke through Ranaya's thought.

Ranaya took a deep breath and followed Sharissa out into the halls.

"It's nice to see you looking your status, instead of that of a peasant." Karik's voice pierced the air as Ranaya entered the dining area. He sat at the end of the enormously long table; an elf on each side of him. One was female and the other male.

There were various dishes of food, enough to feed 20 people.

Ranaya bit her tongue to keep from saying something smart in the presence of the elven servants.

How dare that man!

She stood in the doorway not knowing where to sit. She certainly didn't want to sit by Karik or anywhere close. Not that she had a choice in the matter.

"Well, don't just stand there! Sit down!" Karik said as if she were a dog. He jerked his arm toward the table violently, gesturing for her to sit.

The elves standing around him were looking wary.

Ranaya glared at the King for a moment.

The glances she got from the elves convinced her to sit or there was most likely to be more trouble.

She plopped down two chairs away from him on his right side.

"There, now. That wasn't so hard now was it?" Karik's voice mocked her.

Ranaya held her chin high, looking everywhere but his direction, "Of course not."

The maid on Karik's left dipped food from different platters in Ranaya's plate.

"Thank you," Ranaya smiled politely, and the maid looked surprised but pleased. The elf nodded and smiled back.

Karik tapped his fingers onto the table top. "I'm waiting." He glared at Ranaya for thanking his slaves.

The elf who had just served Ranaya quickly served Karik as if she couldn't be fast enough.

Karik snapped and the other elf that had been standing on his right came to life. The elf made his way to the table and grabbed the glass bottle, skillfully popping off the cork with one hand. He poured wine into Karik's glass first and afterward walked to Ranaya's side.

Ranaya kept her gaze on her plate.

"There you are milady." The elf announced.

Ranaya looked up and fought back a gasp. He looked so familiar it shocked her.

The elf before her looked like an older version of Lando with green eyes.

"Oh," the gasp she had been trying to hold back escaped.

The elf blinked and looked confused. "Is everything all right, milady?"

Ranaya forced her mouth to form words. She was so stunned she barely could move her lips to pronounce the words. "You look like someone I knew."

Karik scoffed, "The eldest brother of the wanted warrior Landrian."

Ranaya's eyes were wide in surprise. It couldn't be! Lando had not mentioned a brother.

The elf shifted uncomfortably at the mention of Landrian.

Ranaya made herself promise to find this elf and talk to him when it was possible. She needed answers.

"My name is Naylandi," the elf said, disappearing out of the dining hall, the female following behind.

Ranaya was speechless.

Lando groaned. He felt as if he had something heavy on top of him.

His eyelids were just as heavy as he forced them open. To his surprise there was nothing on top him at all.

As he took in his surroundings, he realized he was in a cottage.

"How are you feeling?" a familiar voice sounded beside him.

Lando turned his head to see Harry sitting beside him, with a worried look.

"Weak as if my limbs are made of lead."

"I know what you are." Harry didn't look at him.

Lando stiffened then. "Are you going to turn me in?"

Harry furrowed his brows, "I do not see why there is so much persecution among the elves. I have no desire to turn you in."

"I am truly grateful." Lando was touched. He tried to sit up but failed miserably as his head fell back.

"I'm afraid you're very weak." Harry warned as he helped Lando prop up upon some pillows. "You do not have any type of sickness. Your body is simply failing you."

"I knew this would happen soon. I could feel it." Lando closed his eyes and sighed.

"You love her so much," Harry said. "When she was taken, it caused great sorrow to you to even think about it and then when she left it was too much. I have studied on books about your kind. An elf can be so sorrowed the feeling consumes him to the point it kills him."

"I'm afraid my life on this earth is short. My only hope is for Ranaya to come back or go to the Tarachi Forest where I can try to heal." Lando winced as his heart began to spasm.

"I will help you leave the gates of Lakishea, but I'm afraid I cannot travel to the Tarachi Forest. It is no place for a human man. My family needs me to be here." Harry announced, "I can give you a horse."

"Bless you, Harry. I do not deserve your kindness," Lando exclaimed.

"Nonsense. A true friend never leaves a friend in need." Harry smiled.

# Chapter 12

"Your Highness, the King will be mightily upset if you soak yourself!" Sharissa exclaimed with wide eyes as Ranaya lifted her skirts to wade in the water.

It was three days since Ranaya arrived in Zachavi.

Sharissa had invited to show the princess around, outside the castle. Ranaya had been stuck inside for too long and needed the fresh air.

Ranaya had been delighted to see a lake. Immediately she had run to it.

"I do not care what he thinks. I want to have some fun." She quickly walked into the water. It wasn't long until she was waist deep.

"Milady!" Sharissa cried out.

"Come join me," Ranaya insisted with a grin as she let herself sink until nothing but her head appeared above water.

Her fear of water was gone thanks to Lando. She felt drawn to it now. The water made her feel closer to him. She wanted to feel as close to him as was possible if that meant doing things that made her remember memories. But as always, every happy thought of him was interrupted with disturbing visions of him lying motionless on the cobblestones.

She then felt sick, wondering if Lando was better or worse.

"I'd love to but I'm afraid of being punished." Sharissa sat down cross legged to watch Ranaya swim. The elf then noticed Ranaya's forlorn expression. "Are you all right?"

Ranaya sighed, "Before I left Lakishea, a few days before Lando was sick. He didn't admit it but I could tell he was ill. When I was leaving to come here he collapsed to the ground. He looked as if he were inches from death. I worry about him." She lay back until she was floating on her back.

Sharissa sighed, "There was a reason he never told you he was sick."

"What do you mean?" Ranaya asked with small frown.

"When an elf is greatly sorrowed by losing someone he or she loves, grief can sicken an elf; no matter how strong the elf is. It's the worst sickness an elf can ever have. Elves don't get sick often. We get what is known as an elvish cold and then there is the sickness caused by great sorrow. It is incurable unless the one the elf loves comes back and accepts him back. An elf's only hope if the loved one does not return or accept his or her love is to go through elven treatments. Only few heal." Sharissa stared at Ranaya as the girl looked stricken.

Ranaya had turned pale, and she sank underneath the water and then came back up sputtering, "You are saying Lando has no cure and will perish if I do not return to him?"

Sharissa nodded.

Suddenly, swimming didn't appeal to Ranaya so much anymore. Instead, she felt sicker than she even had before.

She made her way to shore and flopped down beside Sharissa. "Sharissa, I have to get back to him. I can't let him die."

Sharissa frowned, "You cannot dare try to escape Zachavi now. Karik will expect it. Wait awhile longer and run away when he least expects it."

Silence followed.

"You are right. I just don't want to wait so long. For all I know Lando could die today or the next if he's not healed." Ranaya choked on tears.

"Landrian is a fighter. He will not give up easily." Sharissa assured the princess.

"When I go I want to help you escape with me." Ranaya stood up.

Sharissa gasped in surprise. "You would help me?" she stood as well. "Why bother with me?"

"You have been a great friend to me since I have been here. You deserve to go back to your people." Ranaya smiled at the maid.

"I have nothing to go back to. The Zachavians killed my husband Galan." Sharissa sounded as if she were about to cry herself.

"But you will be with your people." Ranaya protested.

"I suppose you are right. I will no longer be under Karik's thumb."

"Sharissa, how long has Naylandi lived in Zachavi?" Ranaya asked. It had been bothering her ever since she met the elf, who was Lando's older brother.

Sharissa took a sharp intake of breath. "He was one of the first elves enslaved by the Zachavians. He was 100 years old when he was taken; equaling to ten years old to an elf. He was a small boy when Landrian was born. After that, Landrian and Naylandi's parents raised Landrian to become a great warrior among the people. To avenge the capture of Naylandi—only Landrian doesn't know he has an older brother."

"Why doesn't he?" Ranaya picked her way back to the castle Sharissa by her side.

"His parents kept it a secret all these years. No one speaks of Naylandi in the Tarachi, for it is far too painful to speak of. You see, Landrian and Naylandi are both cousins to the Elven Prince. Their father is brother to King Halidad. Since they were a part of the royal family losing Naylandi was a great misfortune. He was to be raised as a warrior; a leader to the other warriors, but it wasn't meant to be. Landrian was the one to have that fate. The Tarachi couldn't have a better warrior. As of late, royalty and warrior status do not matter for our kingdom since our people are broken up. Some are hiding in caves and others pretend to be humans in other kingdoms." Sharissa explained. By now, they were entering the castle doors.

"I promise now and here. I will escape Zachavi with both you and Naylandi." Ranaya was determined to keep this promise.

"Oh, you miserable wench, look at you! What have you been doing?" Karik roared as Ranaya and Sharissa made their way into the halls.

Ranaya was trying her best to sneak into her chamber to change dresses. And at once, Karik who was also walking in the same hall spotted her. Now, he was reprimanding her.

She fought the urge to roll her eyes. Sharissa was looking rather nervous to be in the presence of the angry king.

Karik was still rambling, "Do you know how much that dress cost me? Of all the things I have bought for you. You appreciate nothing. Look at yourself, Ranaya! You have algae all over you. Your dress is covered in green." He was red in the face.

"I am sorry, Karik," said Ranaya in a calm voice. This seemed to make Karik even angrier.

Almost instantly, she face was nose to nose with the king. "Do you not remember what we talked about, during your arrival to the castle? You are to call me nothing but Your Majesty or Master." His hand came to squeeze her throat. As soon as he squeezed, he let her go and pushed her away from him.

"I am sorry, Your Majesty." Ranaya shuffled her bare feet, willing her neck to stop hurting. Karik seemed to notice this now too.

"You have no respect to your title whatsoever! You walk around and do things peasants and slaves would only do. I will make you respect your title. I have a little unpleasant task for you to do." Karik's eyes glinted about something Ranaya wasn't sure if she wanted to know. Whatever he was thinking wasn't going to be fair well.

"What is that, Your Majesty?" Ranaya was getting curious. What was she going to do that would be so unpleasant?

Karik then smirked, "You have just received the task of washing all the floors of the main rooms on the first floor. I expect you to be done by sundown or you will have to spend the night in the dungeon. Let's see how a slave's life suits you, my dear Princess."

Ranaya's mouth hung open in shock. How was she to clean all those floors before sunset? Those rooms were all the size of ball rooms and three in all. It was then; she realized it was Karik's intent on sending her to the dungeon.

"I will help you, Your Highness." Sharissa offered, shattering the silence that had settled over.

"No you shan't. It is the princess's burden to bear." With that, Karik left the two still standing in the hallway.

Ranaya had almost forgotten her sodden dress. "This sure will be an unforgettable experience," she mused, mostly to herself.

Sharissa sighed, "I will lend you one of my servant garbs, so you will not ruin one of your good dresses."

"I have something I can wear. There is no need." Ranaya protested, shaking her head.

"If you can't find anything, my offer still stands." The elf smiled. "I will get you the cleaning tools you need. Pray that you finish so you don't have to go to the dungeon." Then the maid was off.

Ranaya groaned. There was no way she would have those floors done before it got dark. It was impossible.

She stripped herself of her wet garments and made a beeline for her trunk, where all her belongings were.

Ranaya was glad she had brought along some of her older dresses. She left her corset off. She didn't like wearing it and it did her no good while she was washing the floors, except maybe making her pass out in the floor.

She laid out her wet clothes to dry and reluctantly began her way down to the first floors of the castle to begin her task.

*Swish...*

*Swosh...*

*Swipe...*

*Scrub...*

Ranaya had been going at it for hours. Her hands were blistering terribly. Her back was aching. She was only on the second room. It had begun to get dark already. She knew she would not make it by sundown. It was clearly impossible, and of course Karik knew it.

She heard the door open and footsteps sounding behind her. She refused to look up and kept scrubbing. By the heavy and angry footfalls she could tell it was Karik.

She wouldn't let him get the satisfaction of trying to intimidate her into begging against going to the dungeon.

The footsteps stopped in front of her. "You are not finished yet?"

Ranaya didn't answer. He knew she wouldn't be through. Why bother to answer?

"Guards!" Karik turned and called.

Ranaya dropped her rag to glare at Karik's back. It took effort not to stick her tongue out at him like a child.

Two guards came forth and seized her by the arms, shackling her as if she were a criminal.

"Unhand me!" Ranaya exclaimed in rage.

"I said, you were to spend the night in the dungeon if you had not cleaned the rooms I asked you to. Why are you so surprised?" Karik said rather sarcastically as he snapped for a maid to finish cleaning the floor.

"You never mentioned chaining me up." Ranaya struggled. How dare that man! He had some nerve.

She was dragged. They didn't even give her time to use her feet. The next thing she knew, she was thrown in to a dark, wet, and cold cell.

"I cannot believe this," Ranaya scowled, four hours later. She was pacing around in her cell. It was the only thing to do to keep her warm. It was move or become so numb she couldn't feel her toes or much anything else. The last thing on her mind was sleeping, no matter how late it was.

There was nothing in the cell except cold stone that was slimy with something she didn't even want to think about.

Rats scurried here and there around her feet but she ignored them. She wasn't the type of female that was scared of varmints.

"You haven't stopped for hours, milady." A voice sounded across the dungeon. She couldn't see the owner because it was too dark, but the glowing form told her it was an elf; his voice sounded familiar.

"I cannot sit," Ranaya sighed. She stopped to peer through the bars and try to make out the guard she was speaking to.

"I'm sorry, that king did this to you. You did not deserve to be thrown in here as if you were a criminal. You would think he'd be satisfied with just punishing me and my people." He stepped toward her cell and she could see who he was.

"Naylandi?" Ranaya was confused, how could he be a guard when he usually was a wine bearer?

"In the flesh," Naylandi didn't sound very proud. In fact, he sounded as if he loathed himself.

"I didn't know you worked down here." Ranaya mused. Cold was seeping into her bones now that she was being still. She fought back a shiver.

"I have been here for almost as long as I have been alive. Karik has me doing a lot of things and a lot of his dirty work as well. To him, I am his most trusted and hated slave."

Naylandi leaned back against the wall, across from Ranaya's cell. She could see that he looked exhausted. His elvish glow seemed to be dimmer than most. It puzzled her greatly.

"I'm sorry," Ranaya apologized.

"You have nothing to be sorry for, Your Highness. You were not the one that made me a slave." Naylandi insisted.

"Still, I am very sorry." Ranaya gave up standing and reluctantly slid down to the grimy floor of her cell.

"I have not been out of this castle since I was a mere elfling. I haven't seen the trees and sky for 351 years." Naylandi paced around.

Ranaya gasped, "That is so long."

"I barely remember what a forest looks like." Naylandi came back and sat cross legged against the wall across from her.

Ranaya felt bad for the elf. It was a horrible thing for an elf not to even remember what a forest looks like. Forests were their homes!

That night, Ranaya didn't sleep and instead talked to Naylandi the whole night, until at dawn, other guards came to drag her out of the dungeon.

# Chapter 13

"I trust you have learnt your lesson?" Karik asked as Ranaya was escorted out of the dungeon.

"Yes," Ranaya answered sweetly, even though she wanted to spit at him. She knew better than to rile him further.

"Good," the man gave a smirk. His nose wrinkled up. "Please, get out of my sight until you are rid of that awful smell."

Ranaya rolled her eyes behind Karik's back and started off toward her chamber. Sharissa was there waiting for her when she entered.

"I am so sorry you had to endure that horrible place, Milady" Sharissa ushered the princess toward the steaming bath across the room, and helped Ranaya out of her soiled dress.

"It wasn't too bad. I at least had someone to talk to." Ranaya shimmied out of the dress and into the tub with a delightful sigh. "Oh thank you, Sharissa." She had never been so thankful for bathes.

"You're welcome, Your Highness. Who did you talk to?" Sharissa was curious.

"Naylandi was on guard duty last night." Ranaya explained before submerging her head underwater.

"Really?" Sharissa turned pink as she sat down some bath salts near the tub.

Ranaya surfaced and gave the maid a strange look. Why was she blushing at the mention of Naylandi?

"We spoke of many things last night. I failed to mention I knew who Landrian was, or that I am married to him." Ranaya trailed off.

"You should, milady. That is not something you should forget." Sharissa shook her head.

"I didn't forget. I just didn't know how to bring it up." Ranaya grabbed the towel lying on the side of the tub and dried herself off while Sharissa found her a day dress.

All at once, Ranaya felt dizzy and her stomach lurched in the strangest way. She felt like she would be sick to her stomach. Ranaya jumped out of the tub, ignoring the fact she was getting water all over the floor. She fled to the chamber pot and fell to knees where she emptied the contents of her stomach.

"Milady!" Sharissa gasped in surprise. The maid stopped what she was doing to go to the distraught girl.

Ranaya clutched her stomach and shook her head. "I don't know what came over me. One minute I was fine and the next this happened."

Sharissa touched Ranaya's forehead, "You have no fever."

"Please I do not want to see a physician. Karik will find out something is wrong with me." Ranaya wiped her mouth on her towel and slowly stood up, fighting a wave of dizziness.

Sharissa nodded, "I will get Hadassah, who is the physician over the elves. She may be able to treat you. Let's get you to the bed." The elf took hold of one of Ranaya's arms and helped her to the bed where Sharissa helped her into one of the plainer cotton dresses.

"I will be right back, milady." Sharissa announced as she helped Ranaya into the bed.

"All right," Ranaya sighed. Her hand unconsciously clutched Lando's ring as she lay on her side. She wondered where Lando was and how he was fairing.

A few minutes later her chamber doors opened and came in Sharissa with another elf.

Ranaya sat up slowly to not upset her stomach more than she already had.

"Let us see what the problem is." Hadassah smiled and sat down beside the princess. "Sharissa has told me of your marriage to our General Landrian."

The elf felt Ranaya's forehead and checked a many number of things. One time she had even pressed her hand against the girl's stomach.

Hadassah looked very puzzled when she was done. She stared at Ranaya as if she were the most interesting thing she'd ever seen. "There is a glow about you, one that humans do not have by their own selves. You are with child, Your Highness; an elven child. That is the light coming within."

Ranaya gasped, her hands coming to touch her stomach. She was going to have a baby? Not just a baby but in fact her and Lando's child. A half elvish baby.

As soon as delight and joy filled her it was diminished by terror. Horrors of what would happen to her or the child if Karik were to find out filled her mind.

"He mustn't know!" Ranaya cried out.

Hadassah and Sharissa both knew who the princess was talking about.

"What will you do, milady?" Sharissa asked, her expression was full of sorrow.

"Sharissa, we have to flee this place. The quicker the better. If Karik finds out about the child there is no telling what the man will do. We have to get word to Naylandi about all of this." Ranaya pleaded.

Hadassah bowed her head, "It will be a hard escape. If you wish to try I know of a trapdoor that will lead you from the castle."

"Thank you," Ranaya said, feeling very thankful.

"I will go find Naylandi and tell him what has happened and what we plan. Hopefully he will join us. If he agrees we will leave in two moons." Sharissa promised and walked out, Hadassah following behind.

Ranaya couldn't believe it. She was with child.

"What on earth are you staring at girl?" Karik growled in annoyance.

Ranaya was staring at the food on her plate. She could hardly inhale the scent without retching. She was trying her best to look cool, calm and collected.

"Nothing," she looked up and hesitantly placed the fork in her mouth.

"You look sick." Karik tried to sound concerned in front of the slaves.

Naylandi was standing against the wall with another elf.

Sharissa had talked to Naylandi about the escape plan and about Ranaya. He had agreed to run away with them. Tonight would be the night they would escape. As soon as everyone was sound asleep, Hadassah was to show the three the route out of the castle from the kitchen.

Whenever Ranaya ate she took and stored food in one of her dress pockets for their journey while the king wasn't looking. The elves watching her do it would not tell.

"I don't feel well," Ranaya let her fork fall onto the plate with a loud clink.

"Shall I call a physician?" Karik asked, raising his hand to get one of the servants to come over. No doubt to get a physician.

"NO! I mean—I don't need one." Ranaya stammered.

Naylandi's eyes widened, but he quickly covered it.

Karik raised an eyebrow.

"I wish to go to my chamber." Ranaya stood up abruptly.

"I didn't give you permission." Karik informed.

"I wish to go to my chamber and I am going to my chamber." She growled under her breath.

Karik shot up out of his chair then was holding her by the arm rather tightly. "How dare you speak to a king in that tone of voice!"

Ranaya glared up at him. "Let go of me, Karik."

Karik's face darkened at her words.

Ranaya wrenched her arm away ignoring the pain from it and fled the dining hall. She raced toward her chambers. Karik was most likely plotting her punishment as she ran. She was in deep trouble after all she said.

She groaned and sat down beside her trunk; the least she could do now she was out of Karik's presence.

She regretted not bringing her boy's clothes. Dresses would make traveling a nuisance.

Ranaya grabbed her simplest of dresses and Lando's navy cloak. The rest she grabbed were her sword and other little things. She packed them all in a knapsack that slung over her back, her sword beside her, ready to strap to her waist. She hid them all under the bed.

Now all there was to do was wait for tonight and hope they could escape without getting caught.

The chamber doors opened and Sharissa came in with her own knapsack of things. A dark cloak wrapped around it. "May I hide these in here? The slave quarters aren't places for hiding things."

"Of course," Ranaya smiled, taking the wrapped sack and placing it under the bed with hers.

"Thank you, milady." Sharissa smiled back.

"No more milady or Your Highness, we are about to be traveling companions. Call me Ranaya." Ranaya placed a hand on the elf maid's shoulder.

"Very well," Sharissa sighed. "I heard what happened in the dining hall. His Majesty must be very upset."

"Believe me when I say he is more than upset." Ranaya laughed.

Sharissa's expression was horrified.

"It will not matter much longer," Ranaya sat down on her bed and wrapped her arms around her belly.

# Chapter 14

Ranaya laid still in the bed, coverlet over herself. She was clad in her traveling dress and navy cloak. Her sword was attached to her waist. She was impatiently waiting for everyone in the castle to go sleep. She was to meet Sharissa and Naylandi at the entrance of the kitchen.

The waiting was difficult for her. She wasn't known to be a patient person.

Unable to wait any longer after another long 20 minutes, Ranaya got up. She slung her bag over her shoulder and tip toed out of her chamber. She paused outside her door to make sure no one was awake.

When she was assured everyone was fast asleep she ran quietly toward the kitchen, making it there in less than 5 minutes.

Hadassah was waiting against the wall. Naylandi and Sharissa weren't there yet.

The only light in the room was coming off of Hadassah.

"You're glowing child," Hadassah smiled to the princess.

"What?" Ranaya asked confused lifting her hand to eye level. She gasped in surprise. Her skin did have a glow to it. It wasn't as strong as the maid's before her but she was nevertheless glowing.

Ranaya pulled her hood up over her head and smiled at Hadassah.

"If one wasn't certain one would think you were an elf." Hadassah laughed as she handed Ranaya a bag of food and canteens.

Gasps sounded behind Ranaya and she turned to see Sharissa and Naylandi gaping at her in amazement.

"What is the matter?" Ranaya asked them puzzled.

"You're glowing like us!" Sharissa exclaimed in delight.

"I know," Ranaya grinned. "The baby is already trying to make his self known."

"The little showoff," Naylandi teased.

"All right you three, it's time to get moving," Hadassah urged, "Follow me."

She led them all the way to the back of the kitchen and pressed against a panel which slid away slowly at her touch.

"Thank you, you do not understand how grateful I am for your help." Ranaya hugged the maid as the others walked out of the kitchen to the open    air.

Naylandi looked dazed. It had been so long since he had been outside he didn't know how to react.

"It was nothing," Hadassah shrugged her shoulders. "Now go. Before you all are caught and punished."

The three took off at a jog, trying to put as much distance from the castle as they could.

Ranaya never felt so tired in her life. Right now she was so tired she was afraid her legs would give out.

The three had traveled at night and sleep in the daytime to avoid being seen.

They had no need for torches to light their way. Their light came off of each of the travelers.

Naylandi had insisted on carrying Ranaya's pack. At first Ranaya protested against it but then later her back ached and she was forced to let him carry it.

It was nearing daybreak as they were reaching Joined Trees Grove. Sharissa had proclaimed it safe to rest there because the Zachavians steered clear of the place. There was a wall separating the Zachavian and Tarachi Forests; to keep everyone on their side of the forest.

Ranaya, Sharissa, and Naylandi would have to walk through Joined Trees Grove for protection from the Zachavi city. They would walk against the walls until the forest ended and

Zachavi's main gate entrance appeared. There they would sneak out.

"Dear sister, you look exhausted. I think we should stop ahead soon." Naylandi frowned at Ranaya as she stumbled on some rocks. He had called her sister since he learned of her secret marriage to his younger brother.

"We need to keep going. I'll be fine for a few more miles." Ranaya shook her head. She wouldn't be the cause of slowing their journey.

"Ranaya, you are worn out. We need to stop. You're pregnant and get tired easier than us." Sharissa put a hand on the princess's shoulder.

"We can't stop. We have to get past the Zachavian gates." Ranaya insisted.

"Ranaya, we're all tired. A rest will do us good. The sun is coming out and we will have to rest until nightfall." Naylandi shifted the bags on his back.

"That is true," Ranaya sighed.

A few more miles ahead they stopped and Ranaya plopped down against a tree. It didn't take long for her to fall into a dead sleep. Sharissa placed a blanket over her.

Ranaya woke up and was surprised to see the sun setting. Sharissa and Naylandi were sitting beside her eating bread and cheese.

"We thought you would never wake," Sharissa laughed and handed Ranaya some bread with cheese inside.

"I can't believe I slept that long. You two should have woken me up." Ranaya grumbled sleepily.

Naylandi said, "You needed it. Believe me."

Ranaya ate her food then folded the blanket.

They slowly began their way when it became dark.

Ranaya was amazed as they passed the Joined trees in the middle of the forest. It was an amazing sight to behold. The small pool beneath the two twisted trees glimmered in the moonlight. She wasn't aware that she had stopped and was gaping until Naylandi turned with a grin.

"Amazing isn't it?"

"Yes, it is." Ranaya broke off her stare and walked with the two elves again.

"I barely remember it." Naylandi mused to himself. Ranaya could see the sadness in his eyes. She could see a big difference in Lando's older brother now he was free of being a slave. He carried himself differently. Even his glow was brighter than before. Sharissa seemed the same way.

Ranaya felt better too, except maybe for the small aches and pains traveling were giving her. She knew she wouldn't be hurting as much if she wasn't pregnant. Being pregnant took a lot of energy out of you.

Joined Trees Grove was a lot shorter than they had thought it to be, and they were at the Zachavi gates in no time. At this point all they could do was hope they wouldn't get caught.

To their advantage there was one guard, and he was dozing at just the right moment.

They slowly inched their way toward the gates and slid through as quiet as humanly and elfishly possible.

At      last      they      were      truly      free.

# Chapter 15

The three had made good time. They were already in the Tarachi Forest. The next step was to get to the heart of the forest where all the elves lived. If there even were still elves in the villages and not were all hiding.

Ranaya hadn't mentioned it to her two companions, but she didn't plan to stay in the forest with them for long. She needed to get back to Lakishea and find Lando.

The forest made her nervous. All the stories about people going into the Tarachi Forest and never coming out were creeping into her thoughts. She knew she shouldn't be worrying about these things. Especially since she had two elves with her but she couldn't help herself.

Every little sound made her jump several feet from the ground. There were many animals in the forest and would logically explain all the noises, but the girl was paranoid.

Sunlight was streaking through the horizon but none of the three travelers minded. Now that they were out of Zachavi they no longer feared of being caught.

Naylandi kept stopping every few yards to admire the forest which he hadn't been in since he was a child.

Sharissa acted as if she was annoyed with him, but Ranaya could always tell she was fighting a smile. She was happy to see the elf finally happy again. They had been friends as children and played together in these trees.

Ranaya had been surprised when she realized that elves could communicate with animals. She was shocked when birds often landed on the two elves and seemed to talk to them. Both elves had conversed back in a foreign tongue that Ranaya didn't know but assumed it was the language of the elves.

There was still a lot she had to learn about the people of the Tarachi.

Ranaya gasped in surprise as an eagle landed on Sharissa's shoulder and rubbed his head against the elf affectionately.

"Valan!" Sharissa smiled and rubbed the eagle's head. She chattered with the majestic bird before it flew off ahead of them.

"What did you tell him?" Ranaya asked, curious.

"I told him to alert the others of the village that we are coming." Sharissa paused and looked hesitant.

"Is there something else?" Ranaya knew the elf was hiding something from her. There was something in the elf's eyes that told the princess so.

Naylandi shifted uncomfortably. He had no doubt had heard the conversation between the lady elf and the eagle.

"Landrian—is here. He is greatly ill, and it doesn't look he will be among the living much longer. He is fading fast." Sharissa said slowly, eyeing the princess to gauge her reaction.

"No!" Ranaya gasped, trying to take a run to get to the village faster.

"Ranaya, wait! You mustn't be alone! The forest is not friendly to humans!" Sharissa cried out in warning.

Ranaya could hear Sharissa and Naylandi trying to catch up to her but she wouldn't stop running. She couldn't! Lando could die any moment. She had to get to him as soon as possible. He couldn't die! She needed him as her husband. He had a baby he knew nothing about yet. It wasn't his time to die.

She kept running until her stomach cramped strangely and she gasped stopping her race through the forest. Ranaya couldn't risk the baby. She was being given a warning.

The two finally caught up with her.

"You must not run away from us like that!" Naylandi scolded, grabbing both of the girl's shoulders.

Ranaya wasn't feeling like being scolded. Pain was shooting through her body. She squeezed her eyes shut to keep from groaning.

"Are you all right, dear?" Sharissa asked, seeing her pain filled expression.

"I'm beginning to cramp. I shouldn't have run like that. I'm sorry." Ranaya wished anything to rest awhile but knew they had to press on.

Sharissa was about to say something when there was a sudden shout.

They all three stiffened. It was no elf.

At that moment a man wearing rags staggered toward them. He had a crazy look in his eyes. "Go no farther!" he snarled.

Ranaya glared at him, "Who are you to tell us where we shall and not go?"

The man took a step closer to her, and she took a step back.

"Give me your money or you shall pay the consequences." The man was dangerously close to Ranaya.

Naylandi grabbed Ranaya's sword that was hooked to her waist and pointed it at the man. "Leave!"

"Do you even know how to use that?" the man scoffed, "Elf." He spat that last word and spittle flew into Naylandi's face.

"We all know how to use a sword and we're not afraid to show you." Ranaya snapped. She wasn't sure if it was the pregnancy hormones or the fact that the man sounded racist but she was getting furious with this terrible man.

"Oh really?" The man was in her face again. His breath was rancid.

Ranaya glared.

He grabbed her by the throat. "Give me your money!" his hold was constricting.

"I have no money. Free me!" She tried to kick him in the shin.

"Let her go!" Naylandi and Sharissa both said in unison.

The man narrowed his eyes. But then his gaze lowered and Ranaya's heart sank. He let go of her throat, snatching the ring that was attached around her neck. "This is even better."

Ranaya gasped, "No, you can't have that. Give it back!" She lunged at the man but he kept the ring out of her reach.

"My, what a ring, where did a thing like you get such an amazing ring." The man chuckled.

"My husband gave it to me. Give it back!" Ranaya cried out in despair.

"Give it back to her, man of the wilderness." A female voice sounded behind the four.

They all turned to see a beautiful yet dangerous looking elf. She held a sword in her hand and had it pointed toward them. Anyone could tell she was an experienced warrior and swordswoman.

"Who are you?" the man asked, looking annoyed.

"Zahea. I am second in command of the Tarachi Warriors next to Landrian the Great. You will be wise to give the lady back her ring. I have many warriors in the trees surrounding you. They will not hesitate to kill you with their arrows." The warrior said.

The man's face looked stricken with fear. "I will not give up that easily, elf."

Zahea made a command in their elvish tongue and there were all at once 20 elves with arrows drawn taunt against their bows.

The man paled three shades lighter and dropped the ring hastily, taking a run into the trees where he came from.

"Find him," Zahea told the archers before turning toward the two former slaves and human girl.

Ranaya picked up her ring and slipped it over her left hand ring finger. The chain was now ruined. She cradled her hand against her chest for a few seconds and then looked up at Zahea. "Thank you, very much," She smiled.

"No thank you for coming to us, Your Highness. Landrian is swiftly growing more ill and weak every minute. You are the only hope he has to get well." Zahea said sadly. "We can't have our General die on us at such an early age."

"Is the village far from here?" Sharissa asked Zahea.

"Not at all, it is just ahead. I will bring you three there if you follow me." Zahea hand motioned them.

Ranaya's lethargic movements were taken over by an excited spring in her step. She was eager to get to Lando. She was thankful to God he was still alive. There was great hope for him. She knew he would live. God wouldn't take him away from her like this after all they both had been through.

As they entered the gates of the Tarachi village all the elves on their roundabouts stopped in their tracks to glance at the newcomers. Their eyes were wide as they took in the human girl amid the three elves. Sharissa, Zahea, and Naylandi stuck close to Ranaya just in case one of the Tarachians thought she was a threat.

They needn't fear for her safety. The elves' wide eyed stares were full of wonder and admiration not of hate or wariness. Of that the princess was thankful.

"Come, I will bring you to Landrian," Zahea smiled to Ranaya and made a motion for her to follow along.

Sharissa and Naylandi were making their way toward a group of elves.

Ranaya blinked in amazement as Zahea took her up a flight of stairs to a house built into the giant boughs of a large oak tree. Ranaya couldn't imagine how the elves built such buildings in trees. Not one house or shop was built on the ground.

Zahea opened a heavy wooden door and ushered the princess in. Ranaya narrowed her eyes to see into the dark house. Her breath caught as she found an illuminated figure lying on a bed not far from where she was.

Lando lay there. He looked so lifeless. His glow seemed frighteningly dimmer. It was so dull he barely shed any light amidst a few flickers. His skin was so pale and his hair hung limp across the pillow his head lay on.

Ranaya ran to his side and dropped to her knees. "Landrian," she whispered, using his real name. It was time she used it. She took his nearest hand and placed it on her cheek, with a cry. Seeing him like this scared her so much. She had never seen him look so vulnerable and lifeless.

His hand held little warmth to it

"He's dying, Your Highness. He has little time left." Zahea had tears in her own eyes as she left Ranaya beside Landrian.

"Lando? Landrian?" Ranaya cradled his hand against her face, "I ran away my love. I got away from Karik. I'm never going to go back. Do you hear me?"

Landrian's face stayed void of any expression but she kept speaking. Just maybe he would hear or recognize her voice and try to fight this illness.

"Please don't give up yet. Fight this, Landrian. You have to fight. Don't let it beat you. Do it for me and the ba--" Ranaya cut herself off, realizing what she was about to say.

She gasped when she felt him squeeze her hand ever so slight. It was a weak squeeze but a squeeze nonetheless.

Ranaya smiled. So he heard her talking to him.

She tried to fight a yawn but couldn't. She was so exhausted from her trip. She wanted so much to sleep.

Ranaya sighed and before she thought of what she was doing she laid her head down on Landrian. The last thing she heard was his slow heartbeat before blackness clouded her vision.

Something was stroking Ranaya's hair... something like a hand. At first, she thought she was dreaming. She opened her eyes and blinked, still feeling the sensation then knew she wasn't dreaming. There was only one person that was there in the room and that was Landrian. Her heart skipped, thinking he had to be awake.

Ranaya raised her head to look at Landrian. Her green eyes met his blue ones.

"Ranaya," he said hoarsely. He sounded weak, his voice not having its usual musical ability. To Ranaya, she couldn't have heard a more beautiful sound.

"You're awake!" Ranaya cried out. She fought the urge to throw her arms around him and squeeze him with all her might. She hugged him tightly but not enough to cause him discomfort.

"Am I dreaming you are really here beside me?" Landrian mused, hugging her back just as tight. He felt so much warmer now. It amazed Ranaya.

"No, you are not dreaming. This is real. I am here and I'm not going back." Ranaya promised, pressing her lips to his.

Landrian placed his hand against her cheek as if to assure himself that he wasn't hallucinating. "You have no idea how much it pained me to see you forced to leave Lakishea--" he began.

Ranaya shushed him before he could say all the bad things he went through. "It's all over. I will not go back there and you will get well." She smiled, "I love you."

Landrian smiled but she could tell he was going to fall asleep. His eyelids were heavy. "I love you."

"Go back to sleep, you need to gain up your strength. I will be here when you wake up. I will go let the others know you are awake." Ranaya pushed a fallen lock of blonde hair out of her husband's face and kissed his forehead.

Landrian said nothing else, still smiling. His eyes closed, and he was back asleep in seconds.

Ranaya sat there a few more moments watching him. Reluctantly she stood up and hissed to herself from being so stiff. She had been on her knees for hours she realized. Now they were protesting against her.

She made her way back out of the tree house. Sunlight was streaking through the windows. She was glad she hadn't glowed in front of Landrian. Ranaya didn't want him to ask her questions just yet. She wanted to wait and tell him later today or the next when he was feeling better.

Ranaya wasn't sure where the physician's place was. There were so many elves, she wasn't sure who to ask. Self consciously she pulled her hair over her ears. She didn't know why. It wasn't like anyone could mistake her for an elf with her red hair and tan skin. Maybe, if one of them was color blinded, but she highly doubted that anyone was with their great eyesight.

"Excuse me, could you tell me where the physician lives?" Ranaya asked an elf that was passing by her carrying a basket full of vegetables.

The elf stared at her in question for a moment. Most likely questioning herself why the woman before her was human and not elf. "Yes my dear, right across the path there. You can't miss it." She pointed toward an A frame house up in a very tall   tree.

"Thank you," Ranaya smiled and sprinted after the house in an un-lady-like fashion. By the time she had gotten up the stairs she had to take a rest at the wooden door to catch her breath.

She knocked sharply. A few seconds later a tall elf opened the door. If she ever had thought Landrian was tall this elf was even taller.

"What can I do for you?" he looked surprised to see a human standing at his doorstep.

"Landrian woke up not too long ago. He should be checked on." Ranaya explained to the physician.

He nodded, "And who are you, may I ask?"

"Ranaya, Landrian's wife," she smiled as he got his bag and followed her out.

"You're the princess who Landrian fell in love with and was taken away to Zachavi promised to another man?" the physician asked another question.

"Yes," Ranaya said, feeling herself go red in the face. She didn't like the way he said it but it was true. He made it seem more like a scandal.

By this time they were going up the stairs into the tree house Lando was in. Ranaya opened the door and let the physician pass.

Landrian was waking up when they approached his bedside.

"Ah, young Landrian Brightstar, you're looking more yourself. You had us scared, lad." The physician got to work checking him over.

Brightstar was Landrian's last name? Ranaya didn't even know that.

Ranaya Brightstar…

"I do feel better, Nathan. Thanks to Ranaya," Landrian smiled as Ranaya took his hand in hers.

"Everything is looking good. You should be up tomorrow but take it easy. You are still very weak." Nathan told him.

Landrian nodded, "Nothing too strenuous." He promised, but Ranaya could see a mischievous glint in his eyes that meant he might not obey the physician. There was the old Lando she knew. It warmed her heart to see him look and act so alive. It had brought almost physical pain to her to see him lying unconscious on that bed when she had first arrived. She was so relieved.

Nathan turned to Ranaya then, "Thank you for coming back to Landrian. You are the only reason he lives this moment."

Ranaya didn't know how to answer and only bid the elf farewell. It was getting late now.

Landrian was still so tired he didn't even see the glow coming off of Ranaya's form.

He slowly slid to the right side of the bed so Ranaya could lie beside him. He wrapped his arms around her waist and she snuggled close to him. In a matter of minutes both of them were asleep. Both of them having the best night's rest since they had been apart.

# Chapter 16

Ranaya could hear singing through her slumber-like state.   It was very close to her ear, that she was certain. The voice was familiar but it couldn't be him. She was still in Zachavi. Landrian was in Lakishea still--

She opened her eyes, realizing her surroundings. She was in the Tarachi Forest. Landrian was lying beside her and that was him singing.

Ranaya smiled, her back was to him so he didn't know she was awake. Her ear had a tickling sensation because the elf was so close to her. She fought a shiver as it tickled.

The singing stopped.

"I know you're awake, Ranaya."

Ranaya turned around until she was nose to nose with the elf. "Good morning." Her voice was muffled from just waking up.

"You mean good afternoon," Landrian smirked before kissing her.

"Afternoon?!" Ranaya jerked upright in midway kiss.

Landrian chuckled, "Yes."

"Why didn't you wake me?" Ranaya was exasperated only for a moment. She couldn't stay mad at Landrian. She squinted as the sun shone brightly through the small window.

"I thought you needed the extra sleep. You look exhausted. Besides, I didn't wake up but a few moments ago." Landrian explained.

Ranaya didn't reply because just at that moment the sun moved from the window. She froze as Landrian's skin glowed. She knew full well that her's was as well.

Landrian took a sharp intake of breath. Ranaya was cautious to look at him but she did anyway. She hadn't thought she had to explain to him she was pregnant so soon. She wanted to wait until he had fully recovered first.

"Ranaya, y—you're—g-glowing," Landrian stumbled over his words with wide eyes. "How is that possible?"

"I will explain it to you when you are well enough to walk again," Ranaya promised, but she knew he would protest.

"Why until then?" Landrian frowned. He was very curious to know why a human was glowing like an elf.

"It's nothing bad, Lando—Landrian," she caught herself on his name. "In fact it's really good news and I think it should wait until you are well and can walk." She tried telling him.

He must not have been in knowledge of human women who had the glow of the elves. It could only mean they were pregnant with an elven child.

With little of a warning, Landrian stood up stubbornly, trying to prove to Ranaya that he was in fact well enough to walk. He wobbled at first but kept his balance.

"Landrian 'Lando' Brightstar!" Ranaya gasped and got up quickly and grabbed him just in case he was to tip over and fall.

"I can walk and I am quite well. You see?" Landrian kept up his stubbornness. "Now we can go out to the gardens and you can tell me about everything."

"You were more than half dead yesterday when I got here. If I had gotten here just a little later you would be dead right now. How can you be well enough?" Ranaya still held on to him. She was afraid if she let go he would fall.

"I promise you I am fine. Having you come back to me has made me get well very rapidly. Elves heal quicker than humans." Landrian gently took her hand off his shoulder and smiled.

"Let's go to the gardens to talk?" Lando asked again.

"All right," Ranaya gave in. She had never known this elf in front of her could be stubborn. She smiled to herself regardless of being frustrated with her husband.

"I thought you said all the elves were in hiding?" Ranaya mused as her and Landrian walked across the village to where Landrian had said the gardens were.

"All were hiding until recently. There are still elves hiding in the caves, but most moved back into the villages. King Karik has gotten many of the kingdoms to search for us. It isn't safe anymore to live among humans," Landrian explained, his voice tinged in sadness.

Ranaya still couldn't believe her own father bent under Karik's thumb. Surveying the Lakishean kingdom for elves to reveal and punish them for hiding. King Darius Yarkish of Lakishea had tarnished the meaning of the wonderful kingdom in Ranaya's eyes. It was no longer a place of refuge. It was just like all the other kingdoms.

Ranaya didn't know how to respond to Landrian's words. She knew exactly what Karik was trying to do...

"King Karik is trying to drive us all into our villages so he can rid us for once and for all. He knows where we live. He's mad enough to do what the other kingdoms wouldn't. Traveling through the forests of the Tarachi can be deadly if you have no guide."

They stopped outside the gardens. Ranaya took a glance around in amazement. It was so beautiful. There were so many flowers and the entire garden was inhabited with birds that weren't afraid of the people.

Many of passersby were giving Landrian shocked looks as he and Ranaya walked through the main paths of the village.

Last time they had seen Landrian he had been on death's door.

Ranaya tried not to laugh at their expressions. She could barely believe it herself. Lando still wasn't fully recovered. As they were walking he would wobble every so often and trip causing Ranaya to grab hold of him.

"He must kill me too then. I won't leave here unless it's with you. I won't allow that man to kill your people." Ranaya said heatedly. Ever since her pregnancy she had got very emotional. Now was no exception.

Landrian wrapped an arm around her shoulders and hugged her. "I know, and I know it won't be long when the elves plan war against Zachavi. The torment has been going on too long. We will perish being burned in our villages or we can go to war to win and die an honorable death. God is the only one who can help us now."

Ranaya felt tears prick her eyes. It was silent for a moment.

Landrian broke the quiet. "Now what was it you were going to tell me?" he had seen her tears and was trying to distract her from the news.

Ranaya took a deep breath and looked up at Landrian. He stood there watching her, waiting to hear her 'good news'.

He cocked his head slightly to the side, reminding her of a puppy or maybe a bird.

*Stop stalling yourself, Ranaya.*

She sighed, "You should sit down for this." She noted his still wobbly movements.

Landrian gave her a confused look but led them to a bench.

He gave her a smile, "Now what is it?"

"Landrian, I'm—I'm--" *Just get it out Ranaya!* She chastised herself.

"Yes?" Landrian's smile twitched at first then turned into a frown. She knew she was making him nervous the way she was acting.

"We—we're going to have a baby."

Landrian blinked, shooting off the bench. His mouth opened and closed like a fish. "You're with child?" His eyes were wide. A smile was spreading across his face.

Ranaya smiled back and nodded. He looked dazed.

Without warning, Landrian's eyes rolled into the back of his head.

She gasped and grabbed onto him, trying to ease him back on the bench.

Landrian snapped his eyes back open. "We're going to have a baby. We're going to have a baby," he chanted over and over. His blue eyes grew bigger, and bigger as the seconds passed.

Ranaya fought back a laugh of relief. Who knew Landrian the Great would faint at the mentioning of becoming a father.

Landrian was ecstatic after overcoming his shock.

Ranaya was happy he was excited about their baby; he had worried her at first.

"Excuse me. I hope I'm not intruding."

Ranaya turned to see a regal elf. He had the air of royalty about him. He was regarding Ranaya negatively.

"Did I just hear you say you are carrying an elven child?" the elf asked. He leered at her.

"Zandrial," Landrian said with a warning tone. He ground his teeth, "Your highness." He said as if the title displeased him.

Ranaya didn't answer, staring back at the elf. Who was this?

"You are not welcome here, human. The elves do not mingle with the humans. Neither do they marry nor have half-elven children. It is a disgrace." The elf known as Zandrial snarled in her face.

Something in Ranaya snapped, "Who do you think you are? What you're doing is a disgrace! So don't talk about what is." She could feel her hay wired emotions unraveling.

"Rein in your human wife, cousin," Zandrial told Landrian.

Ranaya felt like someone kicked her in the stomach. Landrian is related to this snobbish prince?

"I will do no such thing." Landrian stepped in front of Ranaya to make Zandrial back up. "She's part of the family now. You will be civil." It wasn't a question, it was an order.

Ranaya blinked. Landrian was talking to the prince as if he were his younger brother.

Zandrial and Landrian were glaring at each other for only a moment, and then Zandrial walked away.

Landrian mumbled something under his breath, sitting down on the bench. Ranaya followed suit.

"Landrian, you talked back at him and ignored the fact he is a prince. He could lock you up for that!" Ranaya exclaimed.

He laughed much to her surprise. "He would do no such thing. I am 20 years his senior. Besides we are cousins and what he said to you wasn't true at all." Landrian caught Ranaya in a gentle kiss.

"You're a princess and you never locked me up," Landrian teased.

"That's different." Ranaya smiled, playfully elbowing him.

Landrian sobered, "I am so glad we are together once more. I thought I would never see you again." He brushed his hand against her cheek.

# Chapter 17

"Where is she?!" Karik bellowed in anger, knocking a vase off a near table before slumping down on his throne.

It had been about 3 or 4 days since Ranaya had disappeared with two of his best slaves. Karik would not stop raging about how the princess had made him look like a fool.

All the slaves were getting jumpy around him from all the yelling. No one liked to be around the King of Zachavi when he was in a foul mood.

Karik shot up in his chair no longer slumping. "I know where they had to have gone." He said to himself with a crazy look in his eyes.

The few elves who were standing beside him took a step back without his notice.

"The Tarachi Forest!" He rubbed his hands together, his head filling up with schemes of how to bring Ranaya back.

He groaned in mental concentration, his hands coming up to rest on his temples.

"Are you ill Your Majesty?" one of the human guards inquired who had been standing on his left.

"I need you to bring the biggest and bravest soldier to me," Karik told the guard.

The guard's eyebrows rose up, but he didn't question his king. He turned and walked out of the throne room.

Karik impatiently waited for the guard to come back with the soldier. And finally after 10 minutes they were there.

"Sir Georgian Lamb at your service, Your Majesty." The bulkiest man Karik had ever seen bowed.

"I have asked for your presence because I have a little task for you. Are you brave enough to travel in the Tarachi?" Karik studied the soldier's reaction.

Georgian blinked, "Haven't ever been, but I know what everyone says about it being dangerous."

"I will pay you one hundred pieces of gold to retrieve Princess Ranaya of Lakishea and bring her back." Karik bribed.

Georgian's eyes bulged. "That's a lot of money just to bring back a woman."

"Will you do it?" Karik extracted the gold from his pocket. He twirled the pieces between his fingers, watching the soldier's eyes.

He knew no one could    resist 100 gold bits.

"Yes, Your Majesty. When am I to go?" Georgian agreed.

"Get your pack and horse as soon as possible." Karik smirked. Soon he'd have Ranaya back.

# Chapter 18

"Landrian, there's someone you need to meet," Ranaya said a few hours after their talk in the garden.

"Who?" Landrian questioned, leaning on Ranaya as she led him over to Sharissa and Naylandi.

Landrian was getting tired from a very eventful half day. He knew he should be in his bed resting, but that was the last thing he wanted to do when Ranaya had just arrived.

"It's a surprise, Landrian." She wrapped her arm around his waist.

He grunted in response. He wasn't a fan of surprises.

Ranaya laughed.

"Father is coming home today," Landrian said as they were approaching the two elves.

Ranaya felt nervous about meeting his father. What was he to think of her? Would he approve of his son marrying a human?

"Do you think he'll like me?" Ranaya bit her lip.

Landrian threaded his fingers through hers. "I'm quite positive." He smiled at her.

Ranaya smiled back, looking ahead. Sharissa and Naylandi stood by a patch of dogwoods. Naylandi's back was to her and Landrian.

Sharissa stared at Landrian meekly, curtsying as if he were the prince himself.

Landrian smiled.

"Naylandi?" Sharissa poked her male companion in the ribs.

Naylandi jumped into focus and turned to Ranaya and Landrian. His eyes widened as he saw his brother. "Landrian?" he asked, stepping forward.

"It is I," Landrian said, curiosity filled his eyes.

Ranaya stayed back to watch the union of the lost brothers.

"You don't remember me, but I remember you." Naylandi explained to his younger brother.

"Who are you?" Landrian's attention was fully on Naylandi now.

"My name is Naylandi Brightstar. I am your older brother you never knew about." Naylandi waited for Landrian's reaction.

"Wh—what?" Landrian blinked in surprise.

"Father never told you about me because he thought it was best. I was kidnapped when you were a toddler by Zachavian soldiers." Naylandi went on.

Sharissa took his hand and squeezed it in reassurance. The gesture didn't go unnoticed by Ranaya.

Ranaya fought a small giggle. She had had a feeling about those two all along.

Her giggle was gone instantly when she saw tears appear in Landrian's eyes as he looked up at his older brother.

"I knew somehow that there was a part of my family missing, even before Mother died." Landrian choked on his tears.

Naylandi grabbed him up into a hug.

Sharissa walked over to Ranaya, both knowing the brothers needed time together. The women walked off to explore the village.

It was apparent to everyone that the two brothers would be the best of friends.

Only Ranaya was feeling left out. Almost the whole day had passed and Landrian had been with Naylandi the entire time.

Sharissa tried to assure her it was only because it had been so long since the two had been together. Ranaya tried to reason with herself that she was being selfish. She knew she was. Naylandi had been without Landrian longer then she had.

She had gone back into the tree house and sat on the window sill. It was her first time at the Tarachi Village and already she felt like an outcast.

She stayed there for hours looking out the window, and eventually she fell asleep.

"Ranaya?" she heard her name whispered into her ear. It sounded like Landrian but wasn't she still in Zachavi?

"Ranaya, Father is here. He wishes to meet with you," Landrian tickled her sides.

Ranaya snapped awake and realized her surroundings. No she was in the Tarachi. She should have known that to start with. Why did she always wake up thinking she was dreaming? Sometimes she even thought she was only dreaming that Landrian was with her.

She shrieked in laughter as Landrian continued to tickle her. "Stop it!" she gasped between fits of laughter.

"What do you say?" Landrian tickled her all the more.

"Let me go, pointy ears!" Ranaya cried out, her words making Landrian laugh too.

"No, that's not the magic word." Landrian refused to let up his torture.

"Blondie!" Ranaya threw another playful insult his way. Her arms flailed about trying to un-attach the elf's hands from her sides.

"Not it." Landrian smirked.

"U—un—uncle!" Ranaya gasped out.

"That's the one." Landrian stopped and sat down beside her.

Ranaya squealed as Landrian bent down to kiss her, thinking he would tickle her again.

Landrian snickered. "Father is here. Ready to go out and meet him?"

Ranaya sat up, feeling serious. "Are you sure he will like me?"

Landrian cupped his hand under her chin, raising her head up so he could look her in the eyes. "Don't worry. He isn't against humans just the ones that threaten us. He will like you."

Ranaya smiled in response.

"He'll be overjoyed to know Naylandi has been returned. I still cannot believe I have an older brother. It still seems so unreal," Landrian said, looping his arm with hers.

"I was surprised myself when I realized who he was." Ranaya remembered how long Landrian had been with Naylandi and how he forgot her and frowned. She quickly masked it before Landrian saw.

He led her down the stairs from the tree house down to the crowded village. Everyone was gathered in a circle.

As they got closer Ranaya realized that the elves were gathered around an elf astride a silver stallion.

Ranaya blinked and took another look at the supposedly silver horse and noticed the great sharp pointed horn. She was staring at a real unicorn when she had always thought unicorns were a myth.

She couldn't keep her gasp at bay and Landrian looked down at her and smiled. "That is Adair; he is my best friend and was a companion during war. I let Father use him when I went off to Lakishea." Landrian gestured toward the unicorn.

Ranaya couldn't stop staring at the unicorn and had to force herself to look at the elf who rode him.

Naylandi came up beside Landrian.

"Father!" Landrian called, pulling both Ranaya and Naylandi with him to meet the elf in the middle of the crowd.

"Landrian?" the elf dismounted Adair.

"Yes, Father it is I," Landrian smiled.

The older elf stood there in front of the three. "It feels like ages instead of months, my son." Landrian's father embraced him.

"This must be the lovely Mrs. Landrian Brightstar." The elf smiled before taking Ranaya's hand.

Ranaya was looking for a cold greeting but this had been the warmest she had received yet. She curtsied, stumbling much to her embarrassment.

"It's nice to meet you, sir."

"Call me Landrial, my dear. After all we are now family." Landrial insisted before turning toward Naylandi. "Now who is this young man, Landrian?"

"It's Naylandi, father. The brother you never mentioned to me. He came back from Zachavi with Ranaya and another elf named Sharissa."

Landrial's eyes widened, "My son?"

Naylandi nodded. Tears were clearly visible in both son and father's eyes.

The village was very quiet as they embraced and wept in each other's arms.

"Your Mother would be happy if she were here to know that you are safe and home again."

Ranaya still didn't tell Landrian that she was feeling left out. She knew he was just happy to be back with all his family, but she was feeling more and more alone.

Days past and they seemed to be in a routine of things. Landrian's health was finally to its original state.

Ranaya felt as if she were seeing a new side of Landrian. He seemed happier than ever, she would catch him humming or singing a little tune if she walked in on him. Even when they were walking in the gardens, which had become one of their favorite things to do when they spent time together.

Ranaya's baby bump was getting more noticeable every day. She was glad to not have to wear corsets anymore. Not that she had really needed them to start with. She had gotten quite scrawny due to not eating properly. Now she had gained her weight back with a baby bump to go with it.

"Ranaya please don't question me on why again." Landrian said, trying to sound patient.

"Why won't you let me come with you?" Ranaya asked exasperated with her husband. He was going with some of the warriors to scout the area. Nothing dangerous, it was just a simple ride on Adair.

She missed him so much. He seemed to always be with the warriors or his brother and father. She felt so left out and he kept denying her company.

"I don't think it's a good idea for someone in your condition." Landrian said, he brushed Adair's silvery coat.

Ranaya fought a small scream of frustration. "Nothing is good for my condition when it comes down to you, Landrian Brightstar. What would it hurt to ride with you around the forest? I've missed you Landrian." Why did he have to be so difficult?

"I just don't think you should." Landrian sighed. "It might be dangerous, Ranaya."

"Dangerous?" Ranaya cried out. "Landrian, I'm capable of protecting myself if need be. All I'm asking is to spend time with you. You've barely been around me since the day after I came here. Do you even love me anymore?!" Tears filled her eyes as she yelled at him. She couldn't hold her tears at bay.

Landrian looked as if he was slapped in the face. "Ranaya, I love you more than anything on this earth. How could you even question that?" he tried grabbing onto Ranaya but she kept herself from his reach.

"You've only been with me an hour or less each day besides when we're sleeping at night." Ranaya accused.

Landrian was about to reply when someone shouted close by.

"Soldiers are coming!" the elf shouted just as thundering hooves sounded.

Ranaya felt sick to her stomach. Karik was after her. Forgetting everything she fought with Landrian about she pressed into him in overwhelming fear.

"Prepare attack!" Landrian commanded going into General mode. He mounted up on the unicorn bareback and reached down to pull Ranaya behind him quickly. She locked her arms around his waist as Adair shot forward with just an elvish word spoken to him.

The soldiers were many as Landrian withdrew his sword. There was no time to get Ranaya to safety. The safest place was on the unicorn with him.

Ranaya squeezed her eyes shut in horror as the Zachavian soldiers rushed toward them. She had put all the elves in danger. There was no doubt about that.

"Don't let go of me no matter what." Landrian's voice was tight. "I love you."

"I love you too," she kept her eyes shut tight.

The next thing she knew Landrian was clanging swords with the enemies.

She felt as if she were in a dream… no it was a nightmare.

Suddenly, she felt herself being pulled off the unicorn. She screamed and struggled.

"Let me go! Let me go! Unhand me!" She flailed her arms about like a mad woman; anything to get away from the soldier. She wouldn't go back to Karik. She'd rather die first.

The soldier tightened his grip on her and urged his horse forward.

"Ranaya!" Landrian cried out. He was right behind her and the soldier.

Ranaya had two choices; let herself be taken by the Zachavians or jump off the horse and pray that she didn't kill herself or the baby.

She chose option two in a matter of seconds. She threw herself so quickly that the soldier hadn't had time to pull her back. Ranaya hit the ground hard, shielding her stomach. She cried out from the impact.

Landrian was there in moments and had her cradled against him. "Ranaya, oh please be all right!"

"I'm fine," Ranaya announced, touching his cheek. She couldn't believe she had ever been mad at him. Right now she had never been so glad    to see him.

Her eyes widened as she spotted the soldier coming behind her husband. He wasn't going for her either; in fact, he was going straight for Landrian. She could see it in the soldier's face.

"Landrian, watch out!" Ranaya scrambled away, trying to grab his sword out of its sheath but Landrian beat her to it and stood up.

"I know you!" the soldier spat out. He swung his sword viciously.

Landrian didn't answer and met the soldier's sword. The scrapping metal rang out loudly.

"You're the General Landrian Brightstar. You killed the former kings of Zachavi!" the soldier's eyes narrowed and he struck his sword even harder.

"What if I was?" Landrian taunted.

Ranaya sat back on her heels. She dared not to move. She didn't know what would happen next.

"You're dead, elf," without even a slight hint of what he would do next the soldier swiped his sword up. He was trying to behead Landrian.

Landrian quickly swerved but wasn't fast enough to avoid being slashed in the face.

Ranaya would never forget the sound of his painful scream.

# Chapter 19

The soldier looked stunned at first from what had happened, but quickly recovered and tried to finish Landrian off.

Landrian knew of what the soldier was doing even through his pain and was able to knock the man's sword out of his hands.

The soldier barely had a moment to think before Landrian killed him, stabbing him in the chest.

Ranaya ran to Landrian and grabbed him as he collapsed to his knees.

He groaned and refused to look at her. "I think I need to go to the physician." He sounded dull and that scared Ranaya.

Ranaya gently forced him to look up at her. He winced despite her effort not to hurt him. Tears filled her eyes as she saw his face.

A slash ran down from his left eye down to the middle of his cheek. Blood covered half of his face but she could see the harsh deep line the sword had bore. He was forever marked.

"Oh Landrian."

"It's bad isn't it?" Landrian inquired, pain very evident in his voice though he spoke calmly.

Ranaya nodded and looked around. All the soldiers were down amid a few very unlucky elves.

There was a shout and Zahea ran toward them. "General, you're wounded! We have to get you to the physician quickly." She dropped down beside the two.

Together, Zahea and Ranaya got Landrian to his feet.

"I can walk without aid," Landrian insisted when they tried to get him to lean on their shoulders.

Neither of the women protested and let the elf go ahead of them.

Ranaya could tell he was greatly upset and wanted to be alone. She respected that.

"You were very fortunate for that sword to not have punctured your eye, General," the physician said as he inspected his stitches on Landrian's face.

Ranaya was amazed by how still Landrian kept as the physician had stitched his face. He barely flinched other than tightening his lips. She remembered not long ago Dari had fallen off his horse and cut his arm. When the physician had sewed him up he had screamed like a girl.

She choked back a laugh at the memory earning an odd stare from the physician. She sobered and felt ashamed of laughing in such a serious situation.

Landrian looked up at her peculiarly and turned back to the physician. "Well I'm alive ,and that is what really matters."

The way he was taking all of this was alarming her. It was like he didn't care at all he had just been slashed across the face.

Wasn't it a big deal to the elves to have scars? Elves were known for their great beauty. Surely a scar was a disgrace to them.

"I would advise you to take it easy, General." The physician proclaimed.

Landrian scowled. It was easy to see even with his face bandaged up. "I don't have time to take it easy. I've already spent over a week lying on my sick bed. Now isn't a time for more rest. There is a war out there about to happen." He slid off the exam table before Ranaya or the Physician could help him down.

"But Landrian," Ranaya tried to protest. She knew he had to be in horrible pain.

"I can't do it, Ranaya. My men out there need my instructions. I cannot be idle." Landrian's voice softened as he spoke to her.

Ranaya nodded. He was right in his words even if it wouldn't be good for him. "But please, just rest for this day?" she pleaded. He needed it after all this.

Landrian didn't argue, "Just for today." He sighed in defeat.

Ranaya felt worn out, and she wasn't even the one who had been fighting.

"Well Mrs. Brightstar, while you are here would you mind if I gave you an examination. I hear you and Landrian are expecting?" The physician inquired.

"Yes that's right," Ranaya answered, threading her fingers through Landrian's.

"A half elven child is a rare occasion. As long as I've lived I've only delivered one. It was sadly a devastating delivery. The baby didn't make it. Something went wrong with the mother." The physician had a faraway look about him and it made Ranaya uneasy.

What did he mean something went wrong with the mother?

She frowned, trying hard not to let it show that what he said was getting to her.

Landrian gave her shoulders a reassuring squeeze. "I'll stay and wait for you. You go   ahead."

Ranaya nodded and watched as Landrian went to stand outside.

# Chapter 20

T hree weeks after:

*Fire… There was fire everywhere.*

*It roared in her ears and burnt her skin as she ran. Elves were screaming in pain and horror as houses and buildings went up in flames.*

*"Landrian! Landrian, where are you?!" she stumbled through the mob of frightened elves for her husband.*

*Dread swept through her. She couldn't find him anywhere. Where was he?*

*Shouting was heard in front of the swarming elves and Ranaya fought hard to see through the smoke and flames.*

*Then her breath caught in her throat. There was Landrian surrounded by three Zachavian soldiers. One held a torch while the other two restrained the elf.*

*Ranaya knew what they were doing.*

*Once an elf was touched by fire it spread over their body rapidly; burning them alive. Elves never liked to get too close to fire for that reason.*

*Landrian's face stayed expressionless as the torch got closer and closer to his skin. The torch illuminated the scar across his eye.*

*"No!"*

"Ranaya, Ranaya!" hands shook her awake.

Ranaya's eyes shot open and saw Landrian's glowing form looming over her with worry.

"You were screaming, what happened?" he asked gently.

Ranaya didn't answer. She couldn't just yet. She stared at the wall, fighting tears.

Blast those pregnancy hormones. She cried more than she had her whole life in a week's time.

Landrian seemed to get used to her random moments of tears. He never questioned why she was crying.

"Whatever it was couldn't have been that bad, could it?" Landrian pushed a lock of hair out of her face.

*Nothing could have been worse than that.* Ranaya thought, tears dribbling down her face.

"Ranaya, please?" he pulled her closer to him and placed a hand on her very noticeable baby bump.

She sucked in a breath, "There was a fire," her voice cracked in emotion. "It was Karik's men. They set the village on fire." Ranaya finished slowly.

Landrian's arms tightened around her body. "Is that all?" he didn't sound very sure.

"Three of the soldiers had you and were trying to burn you." Ranaya whispered, keeping her voice level.

Lando's arms tightened around her.

It was then Ranaya had a horrible cramp in her stomach and it was all she could do not to curl up and scream. She bit down on her bottom lip to keep a noise in.

"Ranaya are you all right?" Landrian asked with concern as he felt her tense up as if in pain.

She nodded not trusting herself to answer without crying out in her pain. She laid down and pretended to be sleepy.

Landrian said nothing else but was suspicious as he lay down next to her.

Ranaya could feel him watching her and she tried her best she keep herself composed.

Only when she felt another intense sharp pain and felt sticky did she let out a crying    half scream.

Landrian bolted up at the sound and grabbed Ranaya by the shoulders. "You are not all right. What is going on, Ranaya?"

Ranaya couldn't answer.

Landrian's expression turned horror-struck, "Your light is flickering. What is happening?" his voice shook.

"The baby," she gasped out in pain. Her fingers dug into his arms without realizing it.

"I have to get the physician," the elf was panicked and visibly shaking. He made to get out of bed.

"No!" Ranaya cried out in a panic. "Don't leave me!" she trembled uncontrollably.

"But you're in pain," Landrian tried to argue.

"It's too late the baby is gone." Ranaya shuddered but refused to cry. That never did any good. Right?

"You need a physician. You could bleed to death!" Landrian tried to reason with his delirious wife.

"Please, don't leave me alone. I'll be fine. Just don't leave me. I beg of you!" Ranaya tried but she couldn't stop the body wracking sob that overtook her.

Landrian didn't say anymore and lay back down to enclose her in his arms tightly but not so tight it hurt her.

She buried her face into his chest and cried. He soothed her when the painful spasms hit her.

It went on for hours like this until the pain stopped. It left Ranaya exhausted, and they both fell asleep toward the morning. Both in a very fitful slumber.

# Chapter 21

Ranaya woke up in pain from the aftermath. Arms were wrapped around her snuggly and there was soft melancholy singing.

Tears sprung to her eyes. It was Landrian singing out his sorrow. She couldn't understand his words but she knew he was singing about their lost child.

Ranaya closed her eyes and took in a shuddering intake of breath to keep from crying.

She knew Landrian was aware that she was awake.

They both laid there in the silence of the morning. Neither wanted to face the day that lay ahead of them but it came anyway.

Landrian stopped singing and turned to look down at Ranaya curled up against him. He smoothed some hair out of her face.

She looked up at him and gave a sigh. His scar was shining in the dim light.

Ranaya gave a weak smile and traced his face with her hand. She ran her forefinger across the scar and across his eye.

"It will be better," Landrian promised her.

Ranaya was mortified as a tear rolled down her face.

He wiped it away and got out of bed.

She didn't want to ever get up but Landrian took her by the hand and pulled her up.

Ranaya hurt all over and her legs trembled. Landrian grabbed on to her quickly and she leaned against him for support.

When her eyes caught sight of the bloodied sheets her stomach turned on her and if it hadn't been for Landrian she would have collapsed to the floor.

Fresh tears filled her eyes and she couldn't force back the sobbing cry of despair. "My baby, my baby is gone! My baby!"

Landrian pulled her into his chest and led her away from the mess. After he calmed her down he made her sit while he filled a bathtub with hot water and sprinkled something in it.

Ranaya felt numb and barely saw Landrian as he fixed her bath for her. She scarcely even felt him helping her into it.

Not even hearing him say he would be back when she needed him.

She sunk into the water feeling her muscles relax. Whatever Landrian had put in her water was helping her calm down.

Ranaya forced herself to away the dried blood coating her skin.

Half an hour later Landrian came back to check on Ranaya who was wrapping a towel around herself.

"I called for the physician to come check on you." Landrian explained.

Ranaya nodded.

Landrian had gotten rid of all the evidence of last night and Ranaya was very grateful.

She gave a small smile of thanks as he helped her lay back down on the clean bed after she was dressed.

It wasn't long that the physician came in. Ranaya didn't want to see him but she knew Landrian wanted for her to be checked on.

The elf was kind as he examined her to make sure there was no damage. He didn't speak of the miscarriage in her presence.

Afterward, the physician drew Landrian away to the corner to speak to him in private but Ranaya heard every word.

"Young General, your mate is in a very fragile state. Physically she's fine," the elf clapped Landrian on the shoulder in reassurance. "Unlike elves she will live but she is very depressed. You must help her through it. She will need you."

Ranaya saw Landrian look toward her and she met his eyes. His gaze softened, and then he looked back to the physician.

Landrian nodded with a firm expression.

"I can't help her. Only you can now." The physician said before leaving.

Ranaya didn't want to be around anybody aside from Landrian so he politely told all her visitors they could see her tomorrow.

Landrian let Ranaya stay inside to grieve, but he was determined to get her outside for some fresh air the next day, even if he had to pick her up and carry her. He would not let her grieve until she wilted away.

That wasn't his Ranaya laying there so broken. He was determined to get her back. He was grieving inside himself but he knew not to dwell on their child's death or he could end up sick. He had to help his mate or wife as what the humans called their better half.

He knew he had to get her well soon. Karik and his army would attack sooner or later and he needed her to help him defeat them. Landrian smiled at this thought. Most elves or men wouldn't ever let their mates fight but he wouldn't have it any other way. He knew even if he refused to let her fight she would find a way.

That was his Ranaya, and he would get her back.

# Chapter 22

"Please eat Ranaya. You have to get your strength up." Landrian tried to coax his young human wife into eating the stew he offered.

Ranaya said nothing as her dull green eyes looked straight ahead at nothing.

If she had been elvish she would have died already. It had been two days since the miscarriage and nothing had changed. In fact, Ranaya seemed to get worse not better.

Landrian didn't know what to do with her. He felt helpless.

Ranaya barely spoke a word. She always just laid silent or wept.

"Please, for me?" Landrian pleaded. He was at his wit's end. What was he going to do?

She didn't even look at him.

Tears welt up in the elf's eyes. What else could he do? He tried everything there was possible. Ranaya simply refused to come back to her old self.

Wait...

What if he took her outside to the gardens? They both needed the fresh air. It couldn't hurt to try.

Landrian knelt down on his knees beside the bed, "Jesus, please help me help Ranaya. She has no willpower and I can't help her. Give her strength to go on." He stayed like that for several minutes. It had been awhile since he had prayed.

When he raised his head Ranaya was staring at him. She didn't say anything but he knew it was progress. She only stared but she was looking at him.

"Would you like to go out into the gardens?" he asked her.

Ranaya didn't answer, and kept looking at him.

Landrian got up and lifted her in his arms. She weakly wrapped her arms around his neck and allowed him to carry her outside.

Elves stopped and stared at their General carrying his human mate, wondering what he was doing with the woman.

Nobody questioned him and let him pass.

Landrian didn't stop until they were in the gardens. He placed Ranaya on a nearby bench and sat beside her.

Ranaya kept herself upright on the bench; another improvement. She leaned on Landrian but mostly held herself up.

He had another idea that might help her get back to her old self. A ride on Adair would most certainly do the trick. He was up for anything that would help.

He let her sit awhile before calling out the unicorn's name.

Adair was there not but a minute after.

Ranaya stared at the unicorn in recognition. She slowly extended her hand out and watched as Adair nuzzled it. A slight smile graced her lips but it was gone so quick Landrian wasn't sure if it wasn't his imagination.

He stood up and lifted Ranaya up onto the unicorn's back, swinging up behind her. Adair nickered and took off without Landrian even nudging him.

Ranaya sighed, leaning back against Landrian. The elf behind her kept a steady conversation with the unicorn. She felt lighter than she had in a while. She felt like there was something heavy weighing her down to where she could barely breathe. It was slowly lifting now. Losing their baby was a hard blow. She felt selfish for letting her own anguish take over her. The whole time Landrian had been strong and hadn't let it get to him and took care of her. If he had let the sorrow eat at him he wouldn't even be alive now.

She closed her eyes feeling herself dozing off. She was determined to get through this.

"General!" Zahea's voice rang out behind them.

Adair slid to a stop.

Zahea's face was ashen as she met up to them.

"What's the matter?" Landrian's sensed the urgency.

"Karik's men are planning a raid. They'll be here at nightfall." Zahea looked up to her general for leadership.

Landrian's grip tightened on Ranaya. "Gather the troops. Be prepared to fight."

Ranaya's thoughts were running wild. *A raid?* It was just like her dream. She had to do something. She couldn't just let him fight by himself! She took a sharp intake of breath.

"I'll fight," Ranaya said in a quiet voice. It was too soft for human ears but both Landrian and Zahea heard her.

"Are you sure you're well enough?" Landrian asked gently. He was shocked Ranaya spoke and even more shocked of what she said.

"I'm positive. I can't lay here knowing Karik is coming. Someone has to stop him." Ranaya insisted.

Zahea's eye lit up like a small child in a candy shop. "I have something to give you!"

Ranaya gave a small smile, wondering what she meant by that.

"I'll be back." The lady elf said before disappearing.

Landrian smoothed Ranaya's red hair back. "Are you sure about this? You're barely well enough."

"I need to do this. It will help me. I know it will." Ranaya was determined to fight by her husband's side.

A few minutes later Zahea was holding something that looked heavy. It was covered with a blanket. She laid it down on the ground.

Ranaya was puzzled when she looked up to see a grin twitching across her Landrian's face. "What is it?"

"Get down and see for yourself," Both elves said in unison.

Landrian dismounted and pulled Ranaya off Adair's back.

Ranaya pushed the blanket away. Her eyes widened at the sight before her.

It was a full set of woman's armor. It looked like a perfect fit and was so beautiful. It had been made by the elves.

Ranaya's mouth dropped open. "How?"

"I mentioned you not having any armor to fit you and Zahea decided to surprise you." Landrian explained.

"I was going to give it to you before, but you got sick. It can be a get well present now," Zahea said.

"Well, I guess it's time to practice." Ranaya was feeling like her old self again.

"Let's go," Lando grinned. She was back.

# Chapter 23

Shouting and metal sounded not too far ahead.

Ranaya was ready for Karik and his army. They would not take her or Landrian.

Landrian was tense the entire day. She could understand his guarded manner. He had the whole army's fate in his hands. He was also worried about her. She really wished he wouldn't worry.

Ranaya watched the elf stand still as a statue. His line of vision was trained far ahead on something her human eyes couldn't see.

His lips were moving before she heard his words. "Run, get away from here!" Landrian's voice was hard. It had a sharp edge that set her heart to pound.

"No, I'm staying with you." Ranaya insisted.

He glanced to her grimly. "Are you certain that's what you want?"

Ranaya's eyes flickered ahead and finally saw what her husband saw as they were coming closer. A thousand soldiers were coming. This wasn't a raid, it was an unexpected combat.

Her stomach churned as she turned back to Landrian. "I'm not going anywhere. I'm staying wherever you are. I go where you go. There's no turning back." She took his hand in hers and squeezed it.

Landrian didn't argue. He knew she would stay. He just wanted to make sure this was what she wanted. It was likely one of them or both could die in this fight. He couldn't guarantee she would survive. He nodded before turning to his warriors. A lump formed in his throat.

Ranaya watched as he turned back into General mode. Shouting orders, information, and strategies. She tried to keep herself steady as she saw Karik's men approaching even closer.

Landrian had ordered all the elves to hide and surprise attack at his signal (a birdcall which Ranaya had never heard before.)

He pulled Ranaya behind a gigantic tree to await their attack. Without a word Landrian kissed her hard and long while he held Ranaya's small frame close to his larger one. He was worried for her. He knew Karik wanted her dead just as he wanted him dead. He would try as hard as possible to keep her in his sight.

Landrian didn't let go until it was time to give the signal for attack. Even then, he had to force himself to let go of Ranaya.

Landrian whistled shrilly and straight away the warriors were striking out the enemy, Landrian and Ranaya joining in.

Ranaya furiously slashed at two of Karik's men that came at her on both sides. They seemed to keep on coming; each time she killed a soldier another would follow from behind.

She could hear more than see Landrian taking out many soldiers of his own. She tried not to think about how many elves were falling down dead around them.

The grunts, cries, and screams from both sides plagued Ranaya's mind.

There were too many Zachavians. There was no way the elves would win. She knew it and she could tell Landrian knew it.

Thoughts swirled in her head and she wasn't paying attention. A soldier knocked her to the ground roughly and poised his sword to run her through. Ranaya's sword fell away from her. She stared up in a daze from the impact. She tried to reach for her sword, but the Zachavian's boot came down to pin her arm down.

Ranaya gritted her teeth in pain but refused to make a sound. She tried to kick him with her foot. She had to get him to let go. She struggled, making him apply more pressure on her arm.

This time she couldn't keep the squeak of agony from coming out.

Just as the soldier drew his sword back another soldier behind ran him through. The soldier's face contorted in surprise as the owner of the sword pulled it out. The Zachavian fell forward almost on top of Ranaya who scrambled away and retrieved her sword.

She looked up to see her savior.

Blond hair fallen out of its string, face ashen and smeared with blood Landrian stood with a grim expression. He pulled Ranaya to her feet and disappeared again into the fight.

Ranaya saw Karik fighting his way toward her. Panic filled her. Not once when she was pinned to the ground was she scared. But that man alone had the power to frighten her by just looking at her. It was unnerving. It made her feel weak—and made her hack away harder at the soldiers attacking just so she could get away. Farther back as she could get.

Then again she wouldn't hide no matter what he did. She absolutely refused to cower in that man's presence.

There was shouting ahead. Not ones of pain but of terror. It took Ranaya a few more hacks to realize the Zachavians were taking captives. That must be why Karik was trying to get to her.

She immediately tried to find Landrian and get to him. He was fighting two soldiers. One was burly and seemed to be hard to fight off. He blocked several strikes before making a few of his own. His sword cut into the burly soldier and instantly killed him. The other was taken down by being stabbed in the heart.

Ranaya ran to him. He looked surprised and worried. "They're taking captives!"

His eyes grew huge. "Get out of here Ranaya. Now!" This was his General voice, and he was giving her an order.

"I won't leave you," Ranaya said stubbornly, gripping his forearms.

"You will leave me if you get taken. I can't risk that, Ranaya. That would kill me. Now run! I'm calling for a retreat." Landrian promised and shoved her away.

Ranaya kept herself from turning back to look at him as she ran as fast as she could.

She heard Landrian shout orders of retreat and Karik's loud sinister voice calling back. He would come back by the next full moon with three times the amount of soldiers.

The Tarachians needed more warriors and help--Help from another kingdom.

# Chapter 24

Ten days found Ranaya, Lando, and Halidad Brightstar king of the Tarachi in Lakishea's throne room.

Ranaya was nervous about seeing her parents after all this time.

What would they say to her? Especially, her brother Dari. He knew they loved each other; surely he'd understand of her running away.

There would be scandalous talk of her leaving her betrothed but she didn't care about everyone else just her family.

"Ranaya!" Darius rose up in shock. Helen who looked stricken couldn't rise from her chair. She was several shades lighter than she should be.

Ranaya stepped slowly toward her father, not sure what to expect. Would he be furious with her or happy to know she was alive and well?

"Yes, it's me Father," she turned to look at Landrian beside her, "And this is my husband Landrian Brightstar."

King Darius stared at the elf with an odd expression. Ranaya didn't know what to make of it.

Lando unlike how he was when he was in Lakishea the last time wore his hair pulled back in a string, his elf ears unmistakable now

"You look familiar and not just in name. I've seen you before, haven't I?" Darius asked.

Landrian lowered his head before answering, "Yes, Your Majesty you have—only under a different name. I'm afraid I pretended to be someone I wasn't."

"Pray tell," Darius looked to his daughter and back to the elf.

"I was a stable boy under the name of Lando at one time."

Darius' face went from confusion to recognition and an almost uncontrolled outrage. "You tricked me, made me believe you were a peasant and a human when all along you were an infamous Tarachian General. Do you know that is punishable by death?"

Ranaya gripped Landrian's arm tightly. She could feel his muscles tighten underneath the sleeve of his tunic.

"I am aware," Landrian retorted, looking at the king dead in the eyes.

King Halidad stepped up, "He did it to protect his people, Good King. Surely you must understand. The Zachavians are plotting to abolish us. The elvish race may be only a tale and legend by the next human generation. Our deaths may be very near. We all took hiding places in the surrounding countries excluding Zachavi, only few stayed in our homeland until recently. King Karik is planning war now as we speak. It will be the final war that will end all.

We will either win or lose.

"Your blessing or not Father, I'll be fighting with them." Ranaya included, covering her mouth. She spoke without thinking.

Darius blanched, "You daughter?" his voice pitched in an almost amused and surprised way. "Why, you don't know how to sword fight."

"Yes she does!" Dari shouted in an unmannerly fashion as he walked into the throne room. He came up to his sister and hugged her tight.

"Dari!" Ranaya exclaimed in surprise.

Darius pressed his fingers to his temples as if all this new news was giving him a headache.

Helen rose up to embrace her daughter, over her initial shock at last.

"I should be upset my daughter the Princess of Lakishea can fight a war but I'm not. In fact, I'm proud of you, Ranaya. Very proud." Helen hugged her again.

"I presume you're not just here for a social call, daughter since you brought with you General Brightstar and the King of the Tarachians." Darius asked. He still did not make a move to hug his daughter.

"We are in need of your help, Dear Sir," Landrian said.

Darius nodded. "When has King Karik proclaimed the war to be?"

"By the next full moon they will strike." Landrian looked down at his wife, his grieved emotions evident in his face.

Darius paced the throne room, pondering on the news.

Ranaya hoped he would help them.

Dari looked anxious as he watched their father.

After a few minutes Darius came back and summoned Dari over. He was silent for a moment,

"Tell General Lowell to organize his troops and prepare for battle. I am to write a letter to the King of Toraya to ask for help."

Ranaya felt like jumping up and down like a little girl but refrained herself. Landrian gave her a knowing look as if he knew what she was thinking of doing.

Halidad exhaled gratefully, "Thank you, Your Majesty."

Darius finally hugged Ranaya and could barely let her go afterward, "I am doing this for you, daughter. You are after all are part of the Tarachians now, seeing that you married their greatest General." A small smile graced his thin lips but then dissolved. "Will you ever forgive me for trying to marry you to that horrible man? I was blind to see his true intentions."

Ranaya took his hands in hers, "I already have."

"But I can't forgive you for not inviting me to your wedding."

Ranaya and Landrian shared a secret smile. No one was invited.

# Chapter 25

The next few days involved Ranaya catching up with all her family.

King Darius and King Halidad were busy organizing troops with Landrian, Dari and the Lakishean General Lowell.

Between the war plans, Landrian made time to get to know the Yarkish family. He and Dari were becoming quite the pair. Ranaya had a feeling soon you wouldn't see the one without the other. She was happy the two were becoming fast friends. They were brother-in-laws now. It made her happy that the two were getting along.

Her parents didn't seem to be taking it too hard about her being married to an elf.

Only her father kept apologizing over trying to marry her off to the Zachavian King, Karik Forde.

Ranaya kept assuring him she didn't hold any hard feelings.

She touched her hollow flat stomach where she should have had a baby bump. They were all sitting in the lounge area. Ranaya felt tears fill her eyes. Her baby was gone. Would she even be able to have another one? Maybe her fate would be like that human woman the Physician Nathan had helped.

She couldn't deny that she was frightened. Landrian put his arm around her shoulders. Somehow he could sense her distress.

"Boran, The King of Toraya has sent word. He is sending 1000 of his best soldiers to help fight off the Zachavians," said Darius.

They only had three days before the war was to take place.

Ranaya could tell Landrian was anxious.

Dari was fighting in the war alongside Ranaya and Landrian. He had stubbornly forced the elf to agree.

Ranaya walked slowly through the gardens deep in thought. She thought of life after war if they both survived. What would happen if they weren't able to have children or if they could? There were no real physical differences between humans and elves.--mainly their ears and height. Elve's had a longer lifespan so how long did a female elf's pregnancy last?

Could she dare to hope? She never heard of a half elf. Maybe that was because it was impossible.

"What are you thinking about?" Landrian whispered into her ear before wrapping his arms around her waist.

Ranaya closed her eyes and then turned around to look him in the eyes.

"Landrian, tell me the truth. Am I able to bear your child?"

Landrian's expression darkened, "I can't answer that question. Only God can. I've never known a human woman capable of bearing a half elven child. The baby either dies--or the woman," he said the last part so soft Ranaya barely heard but she caught it.

Ranaya felt herself pale. "I want to bear you a child."

"It might be best if we don't try anymore. It could end badly," Landrian smoothed her hair out of her face.

"I don't care about the risks. If God wants me to have a baby he'll let me without consequences." Ranaya said stubbornly.

Landrian sighed, "I don't think arguing with a redhead will do me any good. You're much too stubborn."

"I promise to do everything you say. I won't argue if you tell me to rest." Ranaya pleaded.

It was only a matter of time before Landrian cracked. He couldn't deny his princess of anything.

"All right we'll try again." He gave in.

Ranaya threw her arms around his neck and kissed him hard. "Thank you!"

Lando responded with an, "Oof!" and fell several steps back. He smiled.

"How about we go to our place and go back to the old days?" Landrian smirked.

Ranaya smirked back before racing into the woods. Of course, Landrian was ahead of her in seconds and left Ranaya panting.

Without warning, he circled back and scooped her up in his arms and ran again until they were at Ranaya's tree.

He put her down and reached for the key around his neck.

Ranaya smiled, seeing he still had it. They dressed in their old armor and grabbed up their swords.

"I'll go easy on you," Landrian teased as they circled each other like predators.

Ranaya scoffed. "Give me all you got!"

"If you say so," Landrian lunged at her.

Ranaya dodged away and made a lunge of her own.

It was like a dance and it was fun.

It was like their first days of being friends, excluding the kisses that were exchanged here and there.

While Ranaya wasn't paying close attention Landrian tackled her to the forest floor and pinned the sword against her metal clad chest.

"Tssk Tssk." He clicked his tongue.

Ranaya didn't move and played dead.

Landrian chuckled, dropping the sword and leaning over her mischievously.

Ranaya didn't open her eyes and give him the satisfaction of being nervous.

It was then Landrian tickled her. She bolted up while squealing and ran.

He caught her easily and undid her armor so he could tickle her sides.

"Mercy! Mercy!" Ranaya shouted while laughing hysterically.

"Mercy you say?" Landrian said with a glint in his eyes.

Ranaya realized they were by the stream Landrian had found and taught her to swim in. Before she could react, she was thrown in.

Water went up her nose and she came up sputtering. "Conniving little pointy eared rascal!"

Landrian just laughed at her weak insults.

Ranaya crawled out of the water and twisted the water out of her soaked dress and tried not to shiver.

The elf was courteous enough to wrap his cloak around her.

Ranaya took her chance and knocked him into the water and raced back to the castle. Knowing she would get payback when he found her.

She hadn't had this much fun in months.

# Chapter 26

One thousand soldiers from Toraya stood in front of Ranaya. It was the day of the war.

General Lowell and Landrian were getting orders together and making strategies with the Torayan General Jazden.

Landrian kept by her side all the day.

Ranaya was happy that he had agreed they would try for another baby. She wanted to give him a son more than anything. She prayed every day. Just maybe  God would allow them a baby.

Ranaya was feeling anxious knowing they were so close to the end. It was the end of the elves or the end of the Zachavians. If this was the end she planned to go down with the elves.

Where ever Landrian went she would go. To the death would they part.

The elves now were her life as much as her family.

"Everything will turn out. I promise." Dari patted Ranaya's shoulder.

She turned to look at her brother, but he was watching her husband and the other Generals talking.

Ranaya sighed, "Yes I know. But I can't help being anxious." She stared at the scar across Landrian's face and was reminded of the soldier who had almost ended him. It gave her fear for his life. Maybe he was the famous elvish General, a legend, but that didn't keep her from worrying.

She wanted this war over. She wanted to begin her whole new life with him. They hadn't been together long enough yet to have to worry about not seeing each other the next morning.

It was cruel, but it was life. Life could be very cruel.

"Whatever happens to me my father will make sure you want for nothing. I promise." Landrian stroked Ranaya's cheek.

Ranaya was horrified that her husband was talking like that.

"Nothing will happen to you. Don't speak such things." She chided.

He sighed. "I'm just saying, just in case I don't make it through."

"We will both make it through. I feel it." Ranaya kissed him and traced her finger across his scar.

Landrian closed his eyes.

"Pardon me, but the troops are ready to march," General Lowell announced, breaking the bittersweet moment.

Landrian kissed Ranaya's hands and slowly let them go. She knew it was hard on him to leave her but they both knew he had to.

She watched him disappear into the sea of soldiers as took her place within them.

They were waiting for the Zachavians to meet them.

Dari stood beside her but said nothing.

She heard horns, signaling Karik and his troops were arriving.

Ranaya took a deep breath and held it as Karik appeared and seemed to stare right at her. His eyes were like sharp cold ice. She knew if he got the chance he would kill her as soon as he would Landrian. The man wanted revenge.

He wasted no time to send his three thousand men after his enemy.

In seconds, there was fighting all around on all sides. A soldier took a swipe at her and she quickly dodged it and jabbing at him. He yowled in pain as her sword went through him and he fell dead.

Ranaya didn't flinch and kept fighting. One by one Zachavians fell but her stomach lurched when she realized some of the Zachavian soldiers were elves being forced to fight against their own people.

It made Ranaya sick. How could Karik do this? He sickened her.

No matter who they were she had to kill them or they would kill her. As much as it pained her to kill them.

So one by one, soldiers fell by her sword.

Hundreds of soldiers had fallen already. The war would not last long if this kept up.

Her blood froze when she turned to see her next opponent was Karik himself. He looked crazy. His hair was wild and his eyes bloodshot. He had an evil smile on his face.

This wasn't going to end well.

"Well, well. What do we have here?" Karik mocked as they circled each other.

"You will not win," Ranaya snarled at him and lunged.

Karik dodged quickly and tssked. "I always liked them feisty."

Ranaya narrowed her eyes and lunged again, clipping his arm successfully.

The Slaves of Zachavi

Karik cried out in pain but didn't stop circling. "It's over."

Before he could take a swing at her another sword swiped it away.

"I wouldn't try that," said a deadly voice of steel.

Ranaya was shocked to see Landrian standing there. His hair was out of his string and blew everywhere, making his warrior stance even the more intimidating.

"Take one more step," Landrian threatened, stepping in front of her. And for once Ranaya didn't get mad for him defending her.

Karik laughed and scraped his sword against Landrian's.

A soldier came up behind Ranaya and she gave him a quick swipe.

It was enough to distract Landrian from Karik.

Karik was closing in on elf. Landrian didn't see but Ranaya saw it and was horror struck.

"Landrian! Watch out!" She screamed.

Karik smirked as he held the sword up ready to slay the elf.

Landrian would not be able to get away this time with only a scar.

269

"No!" Ranaya cried out, not even thinking about the consequences she threw herself between the blade and her husband.

"Ranaya!" Landrian screamed as Karik's sword cut into her side.

Karik looked shocked to see he had wounded the princess and not the elf.

Ranaya felt white hot pain shoot through her side and it hurt just as worse as Karik twisted the sword out of her side. She screamed out in pain, crumbling to the ground.

She had saved Landrian by diving between the sword and the elf....

Ranaya was bleeding profusely.

Landrian gave a warrior's cry before his sword clashed against Karik's. He had the look of pure rage in his blue eyes.

Karik had to take many steps back to avoid the elf's sharp swings

Seeing Ranaya in so much pain by the king made Landrian's movements quicker and powerful. It was only a matter of time until Karik would lose.

Ranaya shook violently and went into convulsions. All she could do was lay there and watch Karik and Landrian fight to the death while trying to stay conscious.

She almost blacked but awoke when she heard an agonized scream from Karik. Watching as he fell forward upon Landrian's sword. Dead, at last.

Landrian wasn't studying his victory and that his people were free. His wife—mate lay on the battle ground floor bleeding to death before his very eyes.

"Ranaya," he drew her up in his arms gently.

She didn't respond and kept shaking.

"Somebody help me!" Landrian screamed.

Dari and Zahea were at once by his side, and bent down beside him.

Zahea quickly ran off to get Nathan.

Lando whistled and Adair appeared. He carefully raised Ranaya on the unicorn's back and led the stallion toward Zahea's path.

And Lando prayed.

# Chapter 27

Landrian didn't leave Ranaya's side for anything.

The physician kept her on his pallet. She was too unstable to move. If they tried she would bleed to death.

He kept applying poultices and the green stuff Landrian had once used for her hand. He wrapped it thickly in cloth.

Ranaya had passed out cold after they had gotten her to Nathan's small medicine hut.

Landrian sat on his knees beside the pallet for hours and never moved.

Dari, Zahea, Landrial, and King Darius knew he was in his own kind of pain.

Nathan had said the sword had missed Ranaya's organs, but she had lost a lot of blood. He had done a transfusion with Dari. Landrian had caught himself saying he would do the transfusion before he thought about it. Elf blood would kill her.

They were only waiting for her to wake up now. And then wait until she stopped bleeding to move her to Landrian's tree house.

King Darius was almost in hysterics when they brought her into the hut. Dari had to calm him down before he had a heart attack.

It was amazing enough that Dari had stayed so calm while everyone else were going to pieces, even Landrian the Elven General of Legend, who was more distraught than King Darius.

"Please, wake up, Ranaya." Landrian stroked her cheek with his long fingers.

Dari and Zahea took the king away so they could calm him down.

Ranaya heard someone calling her name and felt someone stroking her face. It was a very pleasant sensation.

Then she felt a not so pleasant sensation, a horrible painful ache in her stomach.

"Oh, please stop hurting baby. It will be all right." She thought to herself and trailed her hand to her stomach--her flat stomach that was bandaged heavily.

Her eyes shot open in shock. She met Landrian's worried gaze. He looked so worn out. His blond hair was in disarray, and his glassy blue eyes were bloodshot.

"Our baby is gone," Ranaya whispered. Her head was fuzzy. She was delirious. She didn't even know why she said that. It just had come out.

Landrian nodded. He laid his head down on her chest in an embrace and did something he had never done in front of her.

He wept.

"I thought I was going to lose you, Ranaya," his voice cracked.

Ranaya was shocked speechless. He had never cried in front of her. This was very new to her. She wasn't sure what to do.

"I'm f-fine." Ranaya managed, stroking his hair.

Her stomach hurt so much she couldn't help the small noise that escaped.

Landrian rose up. His eyes were misty, and he looked worriedly at the physician. "Is there anything you can give her?"

Nathan's brow furrowed. "I can give her some Willow Bark but there is nothing I can do for her. Try to keep her comfortable as possible."

He gave her the remedy and then walked out so the young couple could have some time alone.

"I'm so thankful you're all right." Landrian kissed her and hugged her with care.

Ranaya closed her eyes, weak in response.

"Ranaya, why did you jump in front of the sword? You knew Karik would strike." Landrian prodded.

"The thought of you dying was unbearable. I can't even think about it. I hardly thought of my motives. Only that I wanted to protect you at any cost," Ranaya looked up at him.

Landrian sighed, "There are none braver than you, fair maiden."

Ranaya felt relief he wasn't mad at her.

Her eyes were feeling heavy.

"Go to sleep. I'll be here when you wake up." Landrian promised.

She did just that and the elf kept true to his word.

# Chapter 28

It had been over six months since the war that had freed the elves out of slavery from the Zachavians. There was no king to rule over Zachavi.

Since Ranaya had been the intended for the deceased King of Zachavi, King Darius and King Halidad agreed on making Landrian and Ranaya the rulers of the failing Kingdom.

The Zachavians agreed on the arrangement. Most of the people had disagreed on keeping slaves. With a new King and Queen they could start over and create new laws to be more like the anti-slave kingdom of Lakishea.

Today was the crowning of the new King and Queen. Only the new Queen was feeling sick.

"Now my dear, please try to sit still," Gertrude chastised the human princess. They were in Ranaya's Queen Quarters in the Zachavian Castle. It didn't look so gloomy anymore. Just having Karik's presence not there seemed to lighten the entire place.

"I need to get to a chamber pot," warned Ranaya. Her stomach was in knots for more than one reason. She was about to be Queen and the other reason…. her stomach felt like it wanted to turn inside out at every strong smell. She felt dizzy too. This had been going on for a month but today it was worse, much worse. She had been trying to hide it from everyone but apparently it was impossible to hide now.

"Hold still just another second," Gertrude fretted, messing with Ranaya's red hair. She was trying to put it up in an elaborate style.

"Gertrude!" Ranaya covered her mouth with one hand and held her stomach with the other. Gertrude came out muffled and somewhat choked.

"Now please dear. You are so impatient. I don't know how General Landrian can stand you." Gertrude huffed as she jammed a pin in Ranaya's head.

"Ow!" Ranaya fidgeted.

The door opened and in came the elf himself. "I heard my wife being tortured and came see what was going on."

Ranaya was about to reply but her eyes widened and she scrambled away from Gertrude, nearly getting her hair ripped out and fell on her knees in front of the chamber pot.

"Lands sakes! You would have spoiled your dress," Gertrude said, utterly horrified.

Ranaya hadn't paid attention to she was only wearing her chemise. All she had noticed was her stomach.

She heaved as all her breakfast emptied out. It hurt to do so. She weakly lay on the floor afterward, not wanting to move for awhile.

"Ranaya!" Landrian ran to her side and gathered her heaped figure. He ignored the smell and held her against him. "Are you all right?"

"I feel dizzy and sick," Ranaya mumbled against his chest.

"I'll go get the physician," Gertrude said and disappeared. "Thank the Lord we brought him with us to the castle."

Lando carefully lifted her up and carried her to the bed and laid her down.

Ranaya closed her eyes. If only the room would stop swimming around.

Landrian dipped a cloth in the wash basin and placed it on her forehead.

"We must cancel the ceremony." Landrian sat down beside her, on the bed.

"N-no. I'll be fine by then." Ranaya said stubbornly.

The elf sighed just as the sun disappeared from the room.

"Ranaya you're so--," Landrian's words faded.

"What?" Ranaya pressed, rising up to see his glowing form. Her breath almost caught.

She would never be used to how even more beautiful he was in the dark. Even with the scar across his eye. How in the world had she ever deserved him?

"You're glowing," Landrian smiled, his eyes sparkled like sapphires.

Ranaya's mouth parted in an 'O' and she smiled in delight, forgetting her nausea. She shot up and hugged him, giving him a kiss.

They heard gasps from Gertrude who had brought in Nathan.

"Well I guess we know what is going on with Mrs. Brightstar," Nathan laughed.

Gertrude looked confused but said nothing.

Landrian stepped aside so Nathan could examine Ranaya.

"W-why is Her Majesty glowing?" Gertrude asked puzzled.

Before anyone could answer, they heard shuffling and rustling going down the hall. The door swung open to reveal Ranaya's mother Queen Helen and Sharissa.

"We heard you weren't feeling well and wanted to see you," Sharissa said, stopping in her tracks to stare at Ranaya like she had two heads.

Queen Helen rammed into Sharissa and stared, her jaw going slack. "What is going   on with my daughter?"

"She's with child, Your Majesty," Nathan bowed rather quick. He seemed a little skittish in the presence of royals. She guessed it was from having an evil king after your people for so long.

Queen Helen couldn't stop staring. She blinked a few times before coming to her senses. "You look like an elf."

Ranaya felt her face burn. She never would look like an elf, but if her mother thought so she would take it as a nice compliment.

Sharissa's green eyes danced, "You're pregnant?!"

Ranaya nodded, trying her best to ignore her upset stomach. She hoped she was keeping a straight and pleasant face.

Landrian took her hand in his, his finger sliding across the ring he gave her.

Dari burst through the door and averted his eyes in surprise. "They're waiting."

"Tell them we're coming!" Ranaya scrambled off the bed, holding her stomach.

Dari left and Sharissa and Queen Helen followed suit, knowing there was to be arguing.

"We should just postpone it. You're not feeling up for it," Landrian tried, following her around.

"I'm fine, really!" Ranaya gave him a green eyed stare.

Landrian stared right back. "Lay back down, please?" he fixed a blue eyed stare, capable of melting ice and making the most stubborn person give in.

Ranaya looked away. She would be had if she stared too long. Elves had that ability about them. Apparently he was trying to use it as an advantage.

Gertrude took a step back and stared back and forth between them with wide eyes, not knowing what to do.

"Landrian, I AM FINE." Ranaya said stubbornly, trying not to look at him.

"But Ranaya," his voice was turning into honey.

*Oh no….*

Ranaya composed herself and gave him a straight face. She got nose to nose with him. Well nose to chest that is. She stared up at him.

"I am going to that coronation if it's the last thing I do, Landrian Brightstar." Ranaya felt herself melting in his eyes. He knew it too.

He sighed, "Stubborn human woman."

"Persistent elf," she bit back with a slight smile.

"Stubborn redhead," Landrian shot back, stooping down.

"Persistent blon--," Ranaya's words were cut off and turned into a muffled 'mmph.'

Gertrude gasped and turned away as Lando kissed Ranaya to block out her next name calling.

It was a kiss that left Ranaya stumbling back a few steps.

"You win," Landrian said against her lips and then helped button her dress in the back, leaving Betsy staring, and Ranaya smiling.

"Always," said Ranaya.

# Chapter 29

Ranaya lay awake. It was in the middle of the night and yet she hadn't fallen asleep. She was restless and her belly was so big it was hard to get in a comfortable position. Every so often she felt a spasm shoot through her. It was twelve months since she was told she was pregnant. For the elves, thirteen months was a full term for the baby to be born. It couldn't be time yet; although her body seemed to say otherwise. They already had names for a boy or a girl.

She wasn't sure if Landrian was asleep. He had his arm draped around her stomach protectively, and hadn't moved in a while.

Ranaya struggled out from under his arm and sighed loudly as another spasm went through her. It was getting sharper.

Landrian made a small noise of protest but nothing more.

Ranaya tried to lay still.

She took a sharp intake of breath as a horrible cramp shot through her and she grabbed her stomach with a groan. She felt something wet go down her legs and a real contraction hit her.

Landrian shot up right away, "What's the matter?"

"Baby wants out," Ranaya winced with a smile.

Landrian got up quickly, struggling to get his clothes on in a hurry.

Ranaya couldn't help but laugh even through her pain. He was so nervous at the thought of being a father and yet he was a King and a General who ruled a Kingdom and fought wars.

Landrian stumbled out of the chamber door without falling and raced out to get Nathan.

The elvish physician had agreed to stay in the castle until Ranaya had her baby and then would return to the Tarachi Forest.

Ranaya was glad he had since the Zachavians knew nothing about half elven babies.

A few minutes later, Nathan came in with Landrian behind looking like a scared child. Gertrude came in as well.

Ranaya patted the bed beside her and Landrian sat down.

Nathan shot orders for Gertrude and some for Landrian and they all got to work.

Ranaya tried so hard not to scream but soon she couldn't keep it in. The pain was unbearable. Not even holding onto Landrian's hand helped.

"Almost there," it seemed like that's all Nathan could say. It was making Ranaya ill and impatient.

There was a baby cry then Landrian was handed a small baby boy, and Ranaya knew it was over--

Only another pain shot through her as she stared at the beautiful baby.

"What's going on? What's wrong with my mate?" Landrian was panicked as Gertrude took the baby from his arms.

Nathan shook his head in worry. "I will have to ask you to leave. I have to find out what's wrong."

"No, No, I'm staying!" Landrian said stubbornly.

"You must go, Your Majesty," Nathan said sternly.

Ranaya was scared and was afraid of Landrian leaving but she couldn't speak or she would scream. Contractions were hitting her again.

What was going on? She had the baby already.

Landrian left, looking torn.

He paced back and forth unable to stop. She had been in there for over an hour and she was screaming like she was dying. He couldn't take this. He had to find out what was going on with her. Wars he could do. Even have his own face slashed, but when it came to Ranaya he just couldn't handle her hurting in any way.

"Brother, you are about to wear a hole in the floor," Naylandi chastised.

Both the Yarkish and Brightstar families were there waiting and Lando was driving them crazy.

He stopped in mid step as another baby cry was heard and Ranaya's screams stopped. He stood there dumbly; his mouth going slack.

Naylandi grabbed him before he sailed sideways in a faint.

Landrian quickly snapped out of it and ran. He stood in the doorway and stared at the picture before him.

Ranaya held two babies in her arms. She was tired but very happy. "Come meet your son Riordan, and your daughter, Lael."

And Landrian did.

## Names of Kingdoms

Zachavi - (Zack-have-vee)

Lakishea - (La-keesh-shay)

Tarachi - (Ta-ratch-ee)

Toraya - (Ta-ray-a)

Glander- (Gland-er)

Irlandia- (Er-lan-dia)

## Names of People

Ranaya - (Ra-neigh-ya)

Elani - (E-lay-nee)

Karik - (Care-ick)

The Legacy of Elwood

Landrian - (Lan-dree-in)

Sharissa - (Sha-ris-sa)

Naylandi - (Neigh-land-ee)

Hadassah – (Hu-des-uh)

Zahea - (Za-he-a)

Zandrial - (Zan-dree-ale)

Adair - (A-dare)

Landrial - (Lan-dree-ale)

Tyrandall - (Tie-ran-doll)

Lael - (Lay-ale)

Riordan – (Roared-in)

After ten years of tears and grit I have finally published my FIRST novel. Believe it or not, Mustang Eyes is actually my second novel. I started this story when I was around eleven. It was thrown away and was rewritten over five years ago. It took a while to find someone besides myself to edit it. My friend, Sarah offered. Bless her for it! So here it is, for you to read! I am starting to rewrite my first novella called Cupid Stallion which I might be publishing in the next year also. I've also started working on Black Wolf, the sequel to Mustang Eyes. I have few others in the works. If you are interested in the others in progress you can email me or find me on my page

Dear Reader, I hope you liked reading the tale of Ranaya and Landrian. If you enjoyed this book please consider leaving a review on amazon. Happy reading!

You can find Emma Rose Lee on her page:

https://www.facebook.com/emmaroseleeauthor

And the cover artist Mel Mather:

http://unicorn-skydancer08.deviantart.com

https://www.facebook.com/melanie.mather

The Legacy of Elwood

*Emma Rose Lee has been writing since she was 7 years old. Her favorite genre of writing is historical as well as fantasy.*

*She loves Native American History, cats, Doctor Who, classic BBC movies, cats, reading, writing, fairytales, Jane Austen, Narnia, and did I mention cats?*

*She lives in a small town close to the eastern coast of North Carolina.*

*She currently has a few books in the works, as well as many fan fictions she needs to update.*